TALES OF A THOUGHT READER

TALES
OF
A THOUGHT
READER

BARRY H. WILEY

ISBN 978-0692472538

ISBN 069247533

I would like to thank Norm Nielsen for his permission to reproduce the Stuart Cumberland Chevalier Poster on the cover which is from his extraordinary collection of posters depicting the history of the conjuring arts. The poster is the only one used by Cumberland in his remarkable career.

A Thought Reader

on His Travels

MR. STUART CUMBERLAND has just returned from a thought-reading tour in Russia and Germany. His talk is of emperors and princes. "Good business?" "Yes. Good business," and the coins fall with suggestive rhythm as he dreamily turns his hand in his pocket.

He tells the following story ...

Pall Mall Gazette, December 30, 1884

THE TALES

Imposibel!

To begin to explain how I became the leading thought reader in Victoria's vast realm requires that I break my basic rule and mention one of my competitors, now dead some ten years. He was an American, a small nervous man about my age with an outrageously frenetic performing style with the somewhat fabulous name of Washington Irving Wellington Bishop.

Back in late 1878, Bishop was the first thought reader to arrive in England and was a sensation from the first. He could apparently detect and act upon the hidden thoughts of total strangers, whether beggars or noblemen. Within only a few months, he needed someone to sort his correspondence and arrange his burgeoning schedule.

So, early in the winter of 1879, I, Charles Garner, had been recommended to Bishop as private secretary by Mr. H. C. Wicks, proprietor of the *Glasgow Daily News.*

I had written several pithy articles for Mr. Wicks' journal on occult themes as the early Hermetic orders, the darker shades of the Kabbalah and such -- a continuing interest, by the bye. The squibs netted me a few extra shillings outside my income as a clerk in Weblin's butcher shop on St. Giles Street, East Oxford.

My working agreement with Bishop was to be a split of his performing profits, 10% --90%, which, as I could count his houses, was more than acceptable. Irving Bishop made the equivalent of two years of my income as a clerk in Weblin's butcher shop in *only one two-hour performance*. A *single week's* income for Bishop, then, was more than I could earn as a clerk *in six years!*

Prominent scientists as Thomas Henry Huxley and Dr. William B. Carpenter had publicly proclaimed that Bishop's powers were beyond normal human experience with Huxley even declaring publicly: "It is well that Mr. Bishop is an honest man, for, with his gifts, he might have been the greatest rascal amongst us."

And what was it that so challenged the two scientists: his thought reading, his exposures of fraudulent spirit mediums -- no, it was a card trick! After Carpenter and his family had engaged in the card trick[1], the prominent scientist even granted the American *the power of Will Compelling,* the ability to compel a person to do something *only through the silent power of Bishop's mind* -- a power that Bishop himself has never claimed!

I am clumsy handling a deck of cards, but even I could see at least 2-3 methods for doing the trick Carpenter described, and in an article a week or two later in the premier scientific journal, *Nature*, a writer explained other methods for the trick. It seems that scientists moving even a half-step outside their specialized area are as simple-minded as the rest of us.

But, it struck me that, like almost all human beings, scientists need something to believe in -- something out there, just beyond the edge of the present world.

---

[1] I have placed a description of the Bishop card trick in an Appendix to this tale. I will leave it to you to work out your own method. The description is taken from the journal *Nature*.-

Closely observing Bishop's exhibitions, I became curious, and began to experiment with thought reading with friends. Within only a few days, I could duplicate some of Bishop's routine, much slower, rougher to be sure, but I felt with experience I could come to match his speed.

Bishop's thought reading was based, while blindfolded and touching the subject in some way, on detecting the unconscious minute tremors of the subject caused by their concentrating on a specific act. Their focusing, for example, on the location of a pin that had been hidden somewhere in a large room.

The blindfolded performer, by mentally halving the room, detecting which half the subject favored, then quickly halving again, and again, the performer could quickly come to close proximity to the hiding place. Then moving his free hand about while sensing the subject's nervous tremors, the performer could soon place his hand onto the pin's location.

I first witnessed Irving Bishop's ability to accomplish this feat in less than a handful of seconds in the vast central hall of the manor house of the Earl of Atherton. The thought reader almost fainted from his exertions. To everyone there, myself included at the time, it was astonishing.

I soon found I could duplicate Bishop's feat — almost as fast –- and without the fainting.

Thought reading, as practiced by Bishop and me, consists of subtlely detecting two things, direction and locality. But with regular, actually more like relentless, practice, truly strange things can happen; as I witnessed in Bishop's inexplicable abilities to detect hidden thoughts sometimes *without* physical contact.

Working for Bishop for three weeks, I collected my agreed share, carefully banked my capital and made notes of his many social and financial contacts. All the while, Bishop was tossing five and ten pound notes around like a farmer threshing wheat. In our fourth week, he short-changed me; in the fifth he disappeared, somewhere north.

I had to return to the butcher shop in East Oxford.

But, I had glimpsed a lucrative life, a life style of which I had never dreamed; but not achievable as mere Charley Garner of St. Giles Street, East Oxford.

#

I wrote Charles Stuart Cumberland again, then crossed it out and wrote Stuart Charles Cumberland on the brown wrapping paper. Yes, that had a better timbre to it -- but the name still needed a bit of a flourish.

"Charley!" John Weblin's voice echoed to the back of the shop. "Lady Metcalf wants her chops!"

I quickly wrapped Stuart Charles Cumberland around the lamb chops, tied the bundle tight and carried it out to the Metcalf butler.

"Quick, quick, Garner. Her Ladyship is expecting her eldest son, Francis, who is returning from two years in India -- and his favorite meal is Her Ladyship's lamb chops."

I gave the package to the ancient liveried butler. I smiled. That worked. My new name and life would be as Stuart Charles Francis Cumberland.

My public yarn would be that my father was a landed proprietor in -- in Leicestershire (far enough away from London to discourage ready inquiry) whilst I had been studying the military, then becoming a journalist until I realized my powers of thought reading.

I could fill in the cracks in the story as the occasion demanded. There was barely any truth in the whole tale, but one big lie is always more believable than a dozen small ones. I had to create and sustain valid upper class credentials to gain entry into the right salons; which meant dressing fashionably, reading widely, while curbing my Cocky drawl. That last has always been the most difficult issue.

And Bishop, being only an American, had no class distinction anyway. But he did have a lot of fruit and nuts. Sorry, a bit of Cockney for a lot of guts.

With my conserved capital from Bishop, I acquired three bespoke suits. Not Savile Row, but close enough for a former journalist.

With the door of the storage shed behind the butcher shop closed tight, I practiced my opening lecture to ensure I didn't stumble into any of the rhyming Cockney slang of my youth. My claimed landed background and scholarly study of the Hermetic and occult arts would stand to flaming ridicule invested with Cockney rhymes.

My first performing venue would be the High Meeting Hall in Luton, far enough from Oxford but within reasonable reach of London. I would be the second thought reader in the Queen's Realm, as I pointed out in my circulars to the London and Luton press, the printing of which, along with the rental fee for the Hall, had exhausted the last of my conserved capital.

Bishop appeared to be out of the way. He was currently being berated in the Glasgow papers, even the *Daily News*, for having filched most of the proceeds from a hospital charity show. Typical Bishop. He thought he could get away with anything. Fruit and nuts for sure.

#

The Hall was comfortably filled. A quick calculation showed I would easily clear over a year's clerk wages. Two reporters from London had identified themselves to me.

Standing backstage, I wasn't nervous. I was panicked. A man doesn't suddenly walk from the back of a butcher shop to the front of a stage with almost four hundred pairs of eyes on him without some sweaty trepidation. But my opening lecture, though halting in places as I had to catch my breath and slow down my words, was received politely.

"Sose, Cumberland, get on wid your'n stuff!" a tall bearded man thundered out from the back, to the rowdy merriment of the audience. "We ain't seen nothin' yet but your'n silly uppity words!"

Even as inexperienced as I was, I could feel the twittering crowd already slipping away from me.

As much as I wanted to tell that bloody beggar what he could do with *his* stuff, I quickly launched into the pin finding routine which came off remarkably well. The shouting audience applauded, the reporters scribbled -- and my confidence soared.

I called forth someone to memorize the serial number of a pound note from his own wallet and, whilst blindfolded, I would search the man's mind to extract the number and write it before the audience on a large blackboard in the center of the stage.

#

Ah, the pin, by the bye, had been placed in the frills of a generously endowed woman, known locally as May the Mountain. When I arrived in front of her after having the subject, an alcoholic sailor who had planted the pin, lead me while blindfolded on a merry journey throughout the hall, May had started to giggle and jiggle.

I had to laugh at myself. The power of thought reading may be a rational attribute, but those few who exercise it are surely walking the edge of lunacy. Cutting chops suddenly seemed a hundred years ago.

As my hand hovered over her vast heaving bosom, the cheering audience was standing to get a better view.

"Don' you get ticklish now, May!" the tall bearded man in back shouted, to the uproar of the audience. "Thought readers can no be trusted!"

May giggled hysterically as she twisted her head to look up at the people standing around her.

Looking down the side of my nose under the blindfold, I sighted the sparkling head of the pin embedded in a satin bow. I continued to move my hand as though about to explore the buxom plateau before me, moving my hand down dangerously close only then to raise it, to the ecstatic squeals of May and the women nearby. Finally, I delicately extracted the pin and held it up to cheers and applause.

But now I was sweating. I could only get two of the five serial numbers on the bill. The audience was becoming restless. The subject, a barrister, just went blank.

I finally gave it up.

"Too goon' for your'n powers, Cumberland?" That familiar raucous voice again. There were jeers from various places.

My closing exploit would be the murder scenario that I had seen Bishop perform faultlessly several times. I had done it six times in practice in Oxford -- but never before in public.

At my request, a committee of three came up to the stage: a clergyman, a banker and an Army officer. I was blindfolded once again; but this time the minister placed wadded handkerchiefs over each of my eyes before he wrapped a black velvet band several times about my head. I could see nothing at all, not even down the side of my nose.

The banker took my arm and led me to a room off the stage while his colleagues selected a victim, the manner of murder and the killer.

Stuart C. Cumberland

I could easily hear the audience shouting, laughing and applauding.

"They will be laying for you, Mr. Cumberland," the banker whispered to me. "The citizens want to see the Christians eaten."

I muttered something faintly intelligent in response, then felt him take my elbow.

Back on stage and holding the wrist of the Army officer, I found the victim within only seconds; a woman two seats into the second row. Just a variation of the pin-finding routine.

The killing was baffling. I passed my hand around the victim but felt nothing.

"Please concentrate, Captain," I said. "Your thoughts are getting away from me."

"I am concentrating," he responded sharply.

I stepped back. "Reverend Martin, would you please take the Captain's place. He is uneasy about the killing."

The Captain jerked his wrist free from my fingers and stomped away.

I reached out with my left hand. I felt someone brush beside me. Martin placed his wrist into my grip. "Concentrate on the manner of killing, sir," I said.

An electrifying sense stunned me. The minister's wrist was alive with intensity. The throat. As I moved my free hand closer to the woman's throat, the stronger was the intensity in the tremors in the cleric's wrist.

As I reached toward her throat, I knew something was missing. She had been strangled, but something was wrong. Then, I realized what it was. I released Martin's wrist and closed both my hands gently around the woman's neck.

"The victim was strangled *with both hands* by the killer," I declared loud enough to reach the back of the Hall. There was an immediate burst of applause.

"Most impressive, Mr. Cumberland," said the Reverend Martin. "But now, sir: Who is the killer?"

I failed completely.

The minister, who only seconds before had been a virtual signpost, went blank, as was the Captain, and also the banker, who had been told the identity of the killer.

I chose not to guess and stepped back. Unwrapping my blindfold, I admitted my second failure of the evening.

The Reverend Martin walked back up to the stage to address the boisterous audience.

"Perhaps it was an unfair test, ladies and gentlemen, as impressive as Mr. Cumberland's performance has been this evening." He gestured toward me. "The killer was the woman herself. She committed suicide by strangling herself. An impossible scenario, perhaps, and thus not a fair test." He extended his hand to me as I mounted to the stage. "But you quickly and correctly sensed the victim and the mode of death, which I dare say was difficult enough.

"My congratulations, sir."

I bowed to the applause.

As the audience was starting to move toward the doors, I glimpsed Irving Bishop near the back, an arrogant smirk on his face. When he caught my looking at him, he tossed his hand in contempt and vanished into the crowds.

I never saw him again.

#

There was no mention of my performance in any newspapers, even in Luton's two free weeklies. Then, three days later, my father discovered a letter from the Reverend Raymond Martin in the London *Times* which extolled my mysterious powers as worthy of scientific investigation.

I had arranged to have mail forwarded to me from White's Hotel in London, so that was given in Martin's letter as my address. Inquiries trickled in -- mostly requests that I donate my "clever talents" to support one charity or another.

But I had an idea that could put me on the news pages of the London press.

There had been an arrest of a Jewish scholar, Samuel Arnfeld, for murder in the East London Docks. Arnfeld admitted he had been near the murder scene, a warehouse on Narrow Street on the Limehouse docks near the Limehouse Cut. He had seen a man running away.

The police had captured Arnfeld as he claimed that he was pursuing the killer. According to the paper, no murder weapon had been found yet, nor had the police described how the murder victim had been killed, nor who the victim was.

Arnfeld's wife publicly pleaded for help for her innocent husband, "a victim of official bigotry".

"So, Charley, whose going to thank you for helping a Jew in East London?" my father asked. "It's too chancy, son. God knows what goes around those docks. And, according to the write-up, that Arnfeld is some kind of mystic or something himself."

I acknowledged my father's concerns. "But if Arnfeld is innocent, Jew or not, isn't that all that matters?"

He looked at me for a moment. "Your late mother's teachings again." He smiled and went back to gutting a chicken.

#

I contacted the Reverend Martin to explain that I wanted to employ my powers to ensure justice in the Arnfeld matter. When we had spoken briefly in his carriage on the way to the Luton train station, Martin had mentioned that his brother-in-law, who also wore the cloth, had a small mission church in East London.

My profits for almost two hour's work had been waiting for me at the ticket office, £68, *cash*, a veritable fortune for any clerk.

As I had walked out of the Hall feeling dangerously rich, Martin had stopped his carriage to offer me a lift to the train station.

#

Rev. Martin's telegram, forwarded from White's, gave Harry Buffett's address in East London.

My play would be a variation on the murder scenario at the police station, with reporters present, to apparently probe Arnfeld's mind to discover support for Arnfeld's claims of innocence which would, I trusted, pressure the police to look further.

That was it. An hour perhaps, a few suitable paragraphs in the press, and then on to more lucrative bookings as I lay siege to the battlements of British upper society.

Not at all the noble venture my father had imagined; and, assuming that Sam Arnfeld was, in fact, an innocent victim of official bigotry, as his wife insisted.

#

Buffett, a tall lean parson with large hands reddened with chilblains, a quick smile across his scarred face, was dressed in workman's clothing, not as a minister. He went as Mr., not Reverend, Buffett. He led me up the steps of the Limehouse district police station.

"Coppers here don't have any patience with interference," said Buffett, "what with the yellow fogs, the Chinamen with their axes, the Jews with their knives, the smugglers with iron clubs, the white slavers, gypsies and all. Many in my, ah, unpredictable congregation have had serious brushes with Her Majesty's justice."

Three reporters, out of the twenty-eight to whom I had sent notes describing what I intended to do, were waiting with their smirks and pencils already in place. After introductions, Ray Mitchem of the *London News* said, "So, Cumberland, you're going to read the mind of ol' Saucy Sam here? Like that American, Irving Bishop?"

I ignored him and advanced to Inspector Alister Hammond who nodded briefly as we shook hands.

"This is a personal favor to you, Mr. Buffett," he said. "You're doing good Christian work in these unhappy blocks. But I've got one mystic back there in a cell, and" -- glaring at me -- "I'm not happy about another coming in."

We walked deep into the rear of the station to the holding cells. Samuel Arnfeld, small, narrow-faced, dark eyed with thinning dark hair, was allowed out of his cell with two Bobbies standing within easy reach. He wore a brown suit with a starched white shirt without a collar.

Arnfeld's wife, an attractive delicate black-haired woman in a worn dress with an obviously new shawl wrapped tightly around her shoulders stood pensively -- as close to her husband as the Inspector would allow.

Hammond nodded to me and stepped back.

I handed Arnfeld a pocket knife. A Bobbie glanced sharply over at the Inspector who only shrugged.

"Inspector, please blindfold me, then have a policeman take me from the room. Once I am gone, Mr. Arnfeld, please hide the knife anywhere in the room. I will read your thoughts upon my return in order to find the knife.

"I do this to measure your mind, sir, to connect, to access it."

#

When I felt Arnfeld's wrist in my fingers, it was like gripping a writhing snake. The nervous energy surging through him was astonishing, beyond anything I had yet experienced.

I found the knife, secreted in the shoe of one of the Bobbies, within a few seconds.

"Now what weapon was used to kill the man? You know do you not, Arnfeld?" I asked, still blindfolded. "That fact was not made public."

There was a moment of hesitation. "Yes," he said with an odd emphasis. "I know."

"Concentrate now on the murder weapon." I didn't know what to expect.

There was a moment of hesitation, then a strange clouding suddenly spread across my mind, paralyzing my thinking, only to swiftly clear.

The tremors from Arnfeld took me to a desk. As I moved my hand, his tremors forced me to open the second drawer down. From under my blindfold, I glimpsed a drawer filled with flotsam. I moved my hand down into the drawer. When my fingers touched a ball of twine there was an unsettling jolt of intensity.

I held up the ball, unwound and snapped off a piece about two feet long. Arnfeld thoughts directed me toward the Inspector.

"The man was garroted with twine, but ... who was the victim?" I stood for a moment. "Mr. Arnfeld, you saw the victim?"

"Yes."

"And did you know him, his name?"

"Yes, Garner," his voice a whisper.

"Think of the victim." Again that clouding effect. I felt led -- even dragged -- to a wall.

I passed my free hand over a bulletin board with papers pinned to it. With the strength of Arnfeld's concentration, I immediately placed my hand on a piece of paper. I glimpsed a wanted bulletin from under the blindfold which had begun to loosen about my head as I perspired from my exertions. Thought reading can be as sweaty an activity as dressing a side of beef.

It was a wanted bulletin about a Chinaman.

Fluttering my fingers to create an occult effect, I said, letting my voice slip and waver, "The victim … the victim, I sense he is not the man described on this poster, but who is also Chinese."

"Correct, Mr. Cumberland," said Inspector Hammond.

"Now, Mr. Arnfeld. The name of the murdered man. May I have a pen? Please pin a blank sheet of paper to the wall that I may write on it."

I heard some shuffling of feet, then Hammond said, "Ready, Mr. Cumberland. What is the dead man's name?"

Like writing the serial number of a pound note, I moved the pen above the surface of the paper, relying on Arnfeld's tremors to tell me when to mark the paper. But, something didn't feel right. I began marking the paper without understanding where my hand was going.

In a moment all tremors ceased.

I pulled the handkerchiefs from my eyes.

My God! I had written in Chinese!

"Zeng Fanzhi. A Chinese doctor and astrologer. Remarkable, Mr. Cumberland," said Hammond. "Remarkable," the Inspector said again, slowly, frowning.

"Remarkable indeed!" said Harry Buffett. "Bless me, Mr. Cumberland, but your whole exhibition verges on the impossible … even, if you will allow me … even on the shadowy occult … the Satanic."

Arnfeld's dark eyes were narrowed, waiting. There was a smile lurking at the edges of his face. But no thought reading was necessary to see the fear in his wife, as she too waited.

There was a moment of silence as all eyes, the reporters, the Bobbies, the Inspector, Harry Buffett, and the Arnfelds all focused on me. Fewer eyes than had watched me in that Hall in Luton, certainly, but more penetrating and unsettling by far.

"Inspector," I said. "I cannot detect any guilt in Mr. Arnfeld's mind." Mrs. Arnfeld eyes glowed with happiness, while her husband only smirked, clearly unsurprised.

Granted, that was something of a stretch, based on a few minutes of thought reading, but the flow of feeling from Arnfeld had been -- well, unrestrained, without any dodginess. There was something about Arnfeld I couldn't finger in my mind; but a guilty man, I thought, would try to mislead, not cooperate.

But, there had been that odd cloudy feeling.

"So, Mr. Thought Reader," said Guy Mordaunt of the *London Truth,* his smirk firmly in place, "who is the killer, if not this Jew?" His mockery continued. "Do your great mental powers reveal that pertinent piece of information?"

The three reporters were grinning ever wider as my face flushed ever hotter.

"I will identify the killer, when there is no threat to anyone." I said. Just blurted out some words to buy some time.

My God, I knew nothing of how to find killers. I only knew how to cut lamb chops.

In all the Shilling Shockers I had ever read, the hero, the detective, usually a Lord or Count or Captain Somebody, found the killer through a sequence of convenient coincidences -- much as having an angel whisper everything into his ear a bare two pages before the story ended.

I had hoped that after a suitable thought reading demonstration, and declaring the defendant innocent, would give me the headlines I wanted; while goading the police to keep looking while I received more bookings at higher prices.

"And, by the bye, Cumberland," said Ray Mitchem. "all this was impressive as the Inspector has said ... but where did you say you studied military matters before experiencing your acclaimed powers of thought reading?" He came closer and whispered in his beer-soaked breath. "I can smell the makings of a Cockney drawl from a mile away. The only military you ever studied, barge Maud, I'll wager, were the rear quarters of the Horse Guards."

Barge Maud = large fraud in Cockney rhyme.

Arnfeld's wife pulled Mitchem away. "Find the real killer, Mr. Cumberland." Her tears smeared over her face. "Find him, please! No one here will lift a finger for Sam. They have enough of what they want, enough to flaunt, to, to hide behind ... to close their *precious* case. There is no regard for truth here." She pressed her hands over her face. "Find him, Mr. Cumberland," she screamed, "or my husband will be murdered in the Queen's name!"

#

There is a certain advantage to ignorance. There are no distractions caused by knowledge and experience. But, as Mitchem had said, if not Sam Arnfeld -- then who -- and why? I had no choice now but to find out, that is, if my fragile new social stature was to be reinforced and those high-paying bookings were to ever appear.

Turning away from his weeping wife, Arnfeld had looked back at me as the Bobbies led him away to his cell. His face was calm, assured. His dark eyes were confident, as if he knew what I was to do, or that I would have no choice.

#

The sun was struggling through the mists when Buffett and I arrived at the dank warehouse. There were dozens of worn and ripped placards and hoardings with Chinese markings pasted across the outer walls.

Zeng's body had been found inside. Inspector Hammond did not know why Zeng had been in the warehouse.

With Arnfeld back in his cell and the reporters gone to their deadlines and the door of his office closed, with only Buffet and I standing before his desk, Inspector Hammond said, "Yes, there was the twine about Zeng's neck. But," he hesitated, picking up a pipe, "I have never seen a strangulation like this one, and neither has the police doctor. A man strangled will struggle, his face will turn blue, there will be deep marks across his throat. There was none of that in this case. But the man was dead." With police medical approval, he had already released the body to Zeng's family. "But he *was* dead," Hammond repeated, his pipe frozen an inch or two from his lips. He shook his head then lit the pipe.

Black-hatted Chinamen in dark tunics and pants quietly hovered in the corners and alleyways along Narrow

Street, as they chattered in a soft singsong murmur. Each man would turn his eyes away each time I would glance at them. But I could feel eyes tracking us at every turn.

"This warehouse is at the edge of the Chinese area. Zeng's body was found there, by that window," said Buffett. "When they arrive, each group, gypsies, Chinese, lascars, Jews, everyone, occupies an area in the Docklands where they can re-establish their culture and beliefs without interference … until they move on. Some church buildings have housed four or five religions. My own church was a Hindu temple two years ago.

"There are sometimes border wars," he added, "that can become vicious. Inspector Hammond and his men have their hands full in Limehouse, believe me."

Other than a plinth of broken empty crates in the corners, the warehouse was empty. Blotches of darkness were scattered across the floor.

"Why would Zeng be here?" I asked. There were dark remnants of a design drawn on the floor, but what I couldn't be sure.

Buffett turned back toward me. Some muffled sounds of passing wagons on the broken street outside...

"Zeng is thought to run a gang which controls some gambling dens, opium smuggling and singsong girls in the Chinese area. He is called a magician by some; and just a thug by others.

"The Chinese have become aggressive in pushing their boundaries. Some even talk of Zeng's connecting with white gangs in Central London."

"Singsong girls?"

"Whores."

I nodded. So what was the Jewish scholar, Sam Arnfeld, doing walking through the Chinese area? Mrs. Arnfeld had insisted to the Inspector that her husband had been lost in the fog that night.

"Buffett, where is the Jewish section from here?"

"About four-five blocks to the northwest, close on to Wapping. Samuel Arnfeld is a respected scholar of the Kabbalah. He's written one or two books on the subject. But, I get very uncomfortable with curious mysticisms of any kind, Jewish, Chinese" -- he chuckled, looking at me -- "and English. The occult is a slippery ugly swamp, reeking of quicksand."

There were only bits of trash where Zeng's body had been found. I wasn't sure just what I was looking for — but that cloudy feeling dealing with Arnfeld — as though it was he who was reading or directing my mind, not the other way.

In one of the articles I had written for Mr. Wicks, I had described an effect that some Eastern occultists could achieve, an ability to confuse the mind of an unwanted intruder, to repel them. Wicks had laughed at my topic as being a bit much, but had said, "The public wants the uncanny, Garner, so keep giving me the uncanny."

As we started back toward the door, a shadow suddenly appeared blocking our egress.

It was a lean Chinaman, young, but with a deeply lined face. A hatchet hung from his belt.

"What you do here?" he demanded. "You Jewmen?" The hatchet was in his hand in an instant. Then he stopped. "You Buffett?"

"Yes. My friend and I are looking into Mr. Zeng's death … to assist the police."

He snorted. "Coppers no care who kill Chinaman. Why you?"

Another taller man appeared behind him holding a hand-scythe whose freshly sharpened edge glittered in an odd stab of sun.

Buffett walked slowly toward the hatchet man, then stopped a few feet short. I was a step to his right, sweating.

"You are Dai Chao, are you not?"

"Heyah, Buffett. How you know Chinaman?" He shifted his shoulders and took a challenging step forward, his hand on the hatchet hardened. The man behind him shuffled forward, too, raising his scythe.

"Two men who attend my church have mentioned your name as a rising leader in the Chinese area."

Dai Chao spat on the floor. "Only rice Christians!" he snapped, but was obviously pleased with Buffett's description of him. "No Chinaman real Christian … only to eat your rice and pretend pray to your gods. This god, that god, what difference?" He took another step, withdrew a black cloth with some white markings on it from his pocket. Dai Chao threw it at Buffett's feet. "This not Chinee. Why it in Zeng's shirt?" His face twisted into deeper hatred. "Jewman kill Zeng. We kill him … or coppers kill him. No matter. Zeng spirit move on. No matter." There was a moment of silence, then the Chinaman stood to one side. "Go Buffett. You try feed poor. You do good ... for a white."

Buffett picked up the black cloth and stuffed it into a pocket.

The body stink that flowed off Dai Chao and his henchman as I passed near them squelched any appetite I might have for a day or two.

#

We had walked about two blocks along Narrow Street into the gathering wisps of fog coming off the Thames that seemed to be gathering strength against a fading sun. Buffett suddenly stopped, just as I did.

A thought had just struck me.

"Arnfeld speaks Chinese," I said. "How could I have written Zeng's name unless he did?"

Buffett started. "My God, Cumberland. That was my thought as well … not a second ago. He must." He stared at me uneasily. "Did you, ah, I don't know how to ask it. But did you, ah, pick up anything from Dai Chao? Any thoughts?"

"I don't speak Chinese, so his thoughts were gibberish to me." An easy defensive answer, certainly. "But his comment about Zeng's spirit seemed more than a statement of respect … more a statement of purpose. Wouldn't you think?"

Buffett was sweating. I had hit home again. But how was I doing this? I was playing hunches, feelings, whatever was crawling around in my mind.

He nodded. "There is someone living near my church who may understand." Harry Buffett stepped closer. He asked in a low voice, "Do you *see* thoughts, Mr. Cumberland ... or do you *hear* them?"

#

Margret Harris was an elderly strong-faced woman. Thinning long white hair was piled in chunks on her head. Wrapped in rags with only two teeth in her mouth, she sat when Buffett pointed to a chair in the back of the dingy pub. But her rheumy blue eyes had come alive with curiosity even before the beer arrived.

"Sose, Mr. Cumberland, you be the thought reader I been hearing about last few hours?"

I nodded, anticipating her challenge: "Sose, read my mind," she would insist. But none came. She only nodded and continued to stare at me, sipping her beer.

There had been a framed faded multi-chrome handbill hanging just inside the door of the pub, Th- Sail-r-s F--end, the sign still managed. The handbill portrayed what must have been a beautiful woman, though the years had worn away most of the detail and color -- except for the name sprawling across the bottom: Sharon de Shannon.

Thought readers, like all gamblers, must understand the odds in a situation, so I took the chance. "You are waiting for me to give you another name, are you not?" I said.

Her smile might have been stunning at another time, but now it was just an open chasm. The coquettish cock of her head was well practiced.

"Sose?"

"Sharon de Shannon?" I spoke the question as a statement, as I had observed Irving Bishop also do innumerable times.

Her eyes and those of Buffett went wide.

"Remarkable, Mr. Cumberland. I feel more uneasy being around you with each passing hour," said the pastor.

Between sips from her mug of beer, Margaret Harris stumbled through her story. Sam Arnfeld, she muttered, did black magick and had a group of followers, muckers she called them, who were killers. Not all were Jews, but all of them were believers in Arnfeld's occult powers. They would appear sometimes at a street corner, come out of the fogs like spirits, then just disappear again.

"Police'ard afraid o'them," Harris said, pushing her empty mug away.

"Why would Arnfeld have been near the Chinese area, in that warehouse?" I asked. "Arnfeld speaks or, at least, understands Chinese."

Harris raised an eyebrow. "He can?" She glanced cautiously around the pub behind her, at the darkening windows, the fogs and night gathering. "They say ... they say he can speak to the Deveel himself," she whispered. "An' so can his little actress wife."

Buffett was clearly shaken.

I felt a creeping uneasiness moving up my spine. I had carefully read several books on the occult and Hermetic practices for those articles last year for the Glasgow paper; but I had no actual experience with pentagrams, spells and such; and I didn't believe any of that confused gibberish anyway.

I was yet new to thought reading, but I had carefully witnessed the willingness, even eager willingness of most people to believe whatever they wanted to believe, to believe whatever illusions that made life livable.

And the fewer facts, the better.

Crossing herself, Harris pulled back from the table when Buffett spread the black cloth recovered from Dai Chao on the table. Letters were written in thick white ink arranged roughly in a square.

MMBAB

BABMM

MMBBA

ABBMM

"What ...?" Buffett started, his eyes wide with fear.

"It is from Aptolcater, the Kabbalistic Master of Adrianople," I said. "June 16, 1724. It is part of a death spell."

I pressed a fist against my lips. My God, I had come across this letter formation in a scroll in a private collection in Oxford. When I had written it up for the *Evening News*, Editor Hicks *had,* after all, asked for the uncanny. I had altered the letters, just to be safe. I had felt silly doing it, but, "Worn next to the skin of the designated life, the black cloth will kill when the same square of letters is written twenty-five times in black ink on a green silk by the adept three hours after the sun sets. The designated one dies within hours, depending on the innate talents of the adept, the victim's face filled with terror. And there are no marks on the body."

Buffett and the woman looked at me with terror in their eyes. Never before had anyone looked at me like that.

"Merciful God, Cumberland," whispered Buffett. "Are you suggesting this was an occult, a black magick killing? The strangulation?" He shivered. "Hammond didn't think that Zeng was actually strangled, even though the man was certainly dead. The evil ..."

I shook my head. I simply didn't know. But something uncanny had been moving in that warehouse.

The dark marks on the floor, like pieces of the Sigil of Samael, maybe? Part of Arnfeld's magick ambush? Zeng's astrology could not prepare him for Arnfeld's assault. And Zeng had been killed late on a Tuesday, the day believed by some to be controlled by the black angel, Samael.

Not even Hicks would publish my article about Samael. He did pay me for my time, however, as he trashed my manuscript.

#

The dark chill was growing as the damp fogs continued to thicken. There were movements, sometimes resolving into definable human beings, sometimes just vague presences.

Buffett had frowned when Harris muttered that she had heard that Arnfeld and his group were trying to take over some of the Chinese territory. For the Chinese to connect with the Wapping gangs, they needed direct access through the Jewish area.

When I handed Margret Harris a five pound note for her help, she refused and wobbled away, muttering to herself about the Deveel's money and dirty black cloths.

After a block or two on Narrow Street, it became apparent that someone was following us. Coming to a corner with a still working gas streetlamp, I nudged Buffett away from the light against a wall.

"Wait," I whispered.

Three forms emerged from the fog. The forms silhouetted by the streetlamp revealed three men carrying a body. They dropped it at the base of the lamp-post and disappeared.

Two steps -- my heart froze. It was Margaret Harris. Her throat was butchered.

"She must have been seen talking to us at the pub," said Buffett, his voice shaking.

No. I realized what I had done. In offering her that damn five pound note outside the pub, I had marked her as giving us something of value. I went cold. I had marked her to be a victim, to be murdered. Deveel's money -- yes, damnit, I had offered her the Devil's money.

There was a green piece of paper with an orange Kabbalistic symbol on it pinned to her shawl, as if a signature.

First, I make a fool of myself declaring Arnfeld innocent; then second, in an unconsidered fit of generosity I mark an innocent woman for murder. Does thought reading render a man progressively stupid?

But now, is my being with Buffett going to mark him?

"We can't leave her remains here, Cumberland, the rats, you know," said Buffett. As though mystically summoned, a Bobbie in a black rain-polished slicker suddenly appeared from the fogs.

Fortunately, he recognized Buffett and accepted our story.

"Oh, yes, and sir, you being the thought reader?" he said to me. "The Inspector has been speaking of you. Most impressed is he. I will look after the lady. The Inspector will have questions for you later."

As we walked away, I stopped and cursed. Buffett nodded at my explanation. I followed Buffett since I had lost all sense of location in the murkiness. Forms appeared and vanished as we walked.

The warehouse was black and empty. Buffett lighted a candle he had been carrying. He carried candles "to light my way to my sinners".

It was obvious. Arnfeld and Zeng were meeting to work out an accommodation between their two gangs.

Fluent to some degree in Chinese, Arnfeld and Zeng could meet alone without interpreters. Meeting in Chinese territory, Arnfeld would be searched for arms -- but not for twine -- nor for a green silk cloth. He must have given the black cloth with white letters to Zeng earlier somehow.

Arnfeld must have drawn the Sigil then, before Zeng arrived. The Chinese would have guarded all doors to the warehouse which provided Arnfeld with unintended protection.

Completing the last of the black letters on the green silk, and with the deed done, Arnfeld walked out of the warehouse as the police approached, which had sent the Chinese fighters running. Almost perfect timing, except Arnfeld hadn't moved quite fast enough. There was the twine around Zeng's neck which he had used to provide a conventional killing means, to temporarily, apparently, conceal the occult aspects of the killing. So, I almost smiled, Arnfeld was arrested for killing Zeng with the twine, when the twine wasn't the murder weapon.

Buffett agreed that scenario made uneasy sense -- but how to prove it?

Each carrying a candle, we each moved slowly, halving the space, and then halving it again, like finding a pin with your eyes open. It was Buffett who found it, a torn piece of green paper with a portion of an orange Kabbalistic symbol on it. Arnfeld must have pinned it to Zeng as an arrogant declaration of war, then it was accidently ripped off when the police handled the body of the dead Chinaman.

Suddenly, I stopped, a cold sweat down my backside. It finally hit me. "Good God, Buffett! Samuel Arnfeld can read minds ... read without contact. He called me Garner at the police station. How could he know unless he actually had read my mind?"

"Garner?"

"My previous name."

We looked around, Dai Chao stood over us with two armed men behind him.

"Heyah, Buffett. What you finding?"

Buffett explained including me in his explanation. Dai Chao nodded toward me. "You Cumberland go back to Inspector? Arnfeld a magickal killer?"

"Yes," I said.

"Why pretend squeeze Zeng throat?"

I said, "To conceal an occult killing, to make it appear like so many killings in Limehouse. To avoid warning others prematurely who may possess the same powers, perhaps." Others. Others? Was I a believer now?

Dai Chao pursed his lips, then nodded.

"You mind reader, Cumberland?"

"Not in Chinese, Dai Chao," I said.

He looked at me in the flickering of our two candles, his flashing hatchet turning idly in his fingers. "You learn our Chinee, Cumberland, you learn to die! With this hatchet, Cumberland." He raised the hatchet close to my face. "This edge … no magick spells!"

Dai Chao turned and vanished.

#

The green silk cloth covered with black letters lay on the Inspector's desk, along with coins, two pound notes and a folding knife. All the contents of Arnfeld's pockets when he had been arrested. The Inspector gingerly handled the silk, his eyes on me. Arnfeld had called it a special handkerchief, a gift from his wife.

"No policeman can believe your story, Mr. Cumberland. You have obviously convinced Mr. Buffett that something sinister is afoot, but judges won't buy an occult killing, even," he hesitated, then picked up his pipe, "even, Mr. Cumberland, if you are right.

"As a result of your efforts, we will investigate the Arnfeld activities more closely, including Mrs. Arnfeld."

#

Two weeks later, I returned to Luton. The milling crowd around the Hall had been drawn by the gaudy criminal publicity of the Arnfeld affair.

As Harry Buffett did not want to be identified in the papers because of possible damage to his missionary work in Limehouse, I exercised that practiced restraint of a politician in puffing my role in the play.

Sam Arnfeld's trial had been marked by unusual chaos as even the magistrate seemed at times to be confused; but eventually, after almost three days of wrangling, the jury brought in a guilty verdict. Arnfeld was sentenced to hang. There was no mention of the occult at any point. His wife had simply disappeared.

Frankly, I would not be surprised to learn that Sam Arnfeld had escaped the rope. I remember that clouding of my own mind only too well.

I had provided the details, with a vague suggestion of the occult, to those three reporters who had originally been present in Limehouse to give them an advance on the other papers; a move which resulted in a ringing article in the *News* by Ray Mitchem which accorded me powers beyond even my own puffery.

The spectators filled the Luton High Meeting Hall to overflowing with dozens standing along the sides. (And all at a higher ticket price, I might add.)

I repeated my original routine with solid success at every point, including getting all the numbers of the pound note (though actually it was a hundred franc note of a French reporter).

And when I placed my hand on the chosen killer in my murder scenario finale, the crowd roared its approval.

Even a familiar voice from the rear was shouting, "Imposibel, Cumberland! Bloody imposibel!"

Note: The death spell described above is genuine. It is written exactly as it was described in the 1724 manuscript.

APPENDIX – W. I. BISHOP CARD TRICK

Upon his arrival in London with his unnamed male assistant, W. I. Bishop, alone, first called on naturalist, physiologist and ardent anti-spiritualist, Dr. William Benjamin Carpenter, F.R.S., to establish his bone fides as a fellow anti-Spiritist by presenting letters attesting to his abilities from prominent American men of science, business and the academic world. Professor Thomas H. Huxley, the naturalist, was also present.

After their examination of Bishop's documents, the American performed demonstrations for the two professors of what Bishop called thought reading, finding a hidden pin, reading the serial number of a pound note and other quick, simple tests.

Intrigued, Carpenter acceded to the American's request for an introductory letter to similarly minded English gentlemen. In the Bishop letter, Carpenter expressed his desire "to obtain for him (Bishop) an assemblage of gentlemen specially qualified to appreciate the importance of experiments of great value to the Physiologist and Psychologist".

But, remarkably, instead of thought reading wonders, it was a Bishop *card trick* that had most puzzled Carpenter, capturing his close attention. Bishop repeated the effect three times with Carpenter and members of his family as subjects with acclaimed success at each occasion.

"I could not," Carpenter wrote later in 1881, "tell how I was led to make the five successive selections of the cards to be taken away, so as to leave behind the card I had originally drawn" He continued, "... this experiment is of great psychological interest, as by showing the large measure in which we may be guided in our choice among things 'indifferent' by *influences of which we are ourselves unconscious.*" (italics in the original).

Carpenter acknowledged that conjurors were known for being able to "force" a choice on a subject, "as Robert-Houdin had forced a card on Emperor Louis Napoleon after Napoleon had deified the magician to do it. The card Houdin forced was the Caesar". However, Carpenter *emphatically denied* that there was any opportunity for the American to play the conjuror.

The effect was a simple one in which Dr. Carpenter selected a card and returned it to Bishop who inserted it back into the pack, shuffled the cards and dealt out sixteen cards *"with their faces downwards"* (italics Carpenter's) in four rows as below:

	A	B	C	D
E	1	2	3	4
F	5	6	7	8
G	9	10	11	12
H	13	14	15	16

Diagram from letter to the editor,

W. B. Carpenter, *Nature*, June 30, 1881.

Carpenter stood at the table with Bishop to his right, and, taking the professor's right hand with his left, Bishop said, "Drop your left hand down on either row, vertical or horizontal, that you want taken away."

This procedure was repeated two more times leaving one row, C, in place.

"Now," said Bishop, "drop down upon either the two upper or the two lower cards of the remaining row." The upper two, 3 and 7, were selected and removed, leaving only 11 and 15 still on the table. "Now drop down on either of the two remaining cards."

Carpenter selected the lower card, 15, which was removed. Bishop gestured at the remaining card, 11, which Carpenter turned over. It was his originally selected card! The scientist was profoundly astonished. Bishop successfully repeated the trick with three members of Carpenter's family.

I sought out the subsequent issues of *Nature* to learn what other scientists might think of the Carpenter/Bishop card trick. My answer appeared in the next issue.

Carpenter's letter, "*Re* W. I. Bishop" which describes the card trick appeared in *Nature* June 30, 1881, p.188. Thomson Whyte of Edinburgh wrote in *Nature,* July

7, 1881, in "*Re* W. I. Bishop", p.211, to describe two methods for accomplishing the trick. The first, the use of two decks with the same back-pattern, in one of which "fifty-two cards are all alike". The second, Bishop tells the subject to "drop your left hand down" on rows and cards without first telling the subject what that action will designate, whether to pick up the row or card, or to leave it. By using the same undefined words at each point, Whyte explains, the operator can subtlely force the subject to the one card he wants the subject to finally land on, assuming that the operator knows the placement of the correct card.

If the operator declares in advance what is to happen when the subject drops his hand, and the correct card is arrived at then, Whyte admits, the result would be beyond normal probabilities. Even better, if neither the operator nor the subject knows the location of the card selected and the correct card is selected, then a special phenomenon has truly been demonstrated.

Whyte complained that Carpenter granted W. I. Bishop the power of "will-compelling", a power that even Bishop himself hadn't claimed. Whyte had seen the

American perform some card tricks in an Edinburgh performance in 1879.

#

So, as the London *Times* printed so succinctly a few years ago:

"There are few delusions that a man cannot be brought to believe if they injure neither his stomach nor his purse."

London *Times,* April 23, 1863

THE HEALING
CLAIRVOYANTE

"Where there is darkness

there is the possibility of imposture;

and the certainty of suspicion."

Daniel Dunglas Home

1877

Lights and Shadows of Spiritualism

Even with Ray Mitchem's flaming article on the Arnfeld case on the front page of the *London News,* that suggested powers for me that even I couldn't explain, the public memory of me as a thought reader faded rapidly as new more scandalous events seized the public attention.

I did perform at three paying venues. Though small they did generate cash for my wounded Stuart Cumberland account. And also performed twice for charity to prove, naturally, what a marvelous chap I was, but the people in those needy neighborhoods scattered at my last bow as though I had just announced a train departure. It was politely explained to me that "as I had not provided refreshments, the spectators needed to look elsewhere for their evening needs".

And that was it.

There were a few more requests from charities of this or that persuasion, all, I am sure, earnest and well-meaning causes. But my prime concern was for my own well-meaning cause. Gutting chickens was rising on the horizon.

Examining the papers and recalling my limited experiences with the American performer, Washington

Irving Bishop, it was clear that the one topic that most gripped the public's mind, *and purse*, was the spirit-world and "the question of the day", as several writers described it: do the departed spirits return from eternity to speak with the living?

It was clear that, regardless of my thought reading powers, if I didn't have an answer for that question, I would not have audiences or gain press coverage. My answer would be, of course, no, departed spirits do not speak to the living. As there was obviously no money in answering yes, I would leave the yes's to the "psychical researchers", whatever that might mean.

I was willing to risk all for the good of the endangered public -- or whatever flutter-finger gibberish that the helpless subjects of the Queen would believe -- to publicly flaunt, to confirm and exploit my superior knowledge of dark fraud. That looked good on the handbill that I wrote, but there was a large gap in the middle: The name or names of the fake mediums I had taken down. I needed a scalp to brandish, to use a colorful American expression. And, it was clear from my bank account, I needed one quickly.

I was also learning that my original plan of first creating and burnishing my Cumberland persona, then, by imitating Bishop, I could tap into Bishop's flow of gold had been, at best, quite naïve. I had only scaled a small foothill with the mountain range still before me, and the clucking chickens gathering behind me.

I began to carefully peruse the personal columns of the principal Spiritualist journal, *Medium &Daybreak*. I came to focus on Mrs. Martha Ann Houghton with rooms at 99, Park Street, Grosvenor Square, who claimed to be a medical clairvoyante and healing medium whose spirit control, Dr. William Harvey, was the eminence who had discovered the circulation of blood back in the sixteenth century. It was Harvey's presence, whose personal control enabled Mrs. Houghton to cure infirmities at a distance with only a lock of the patient's hair at her fingertips. Her at-home hours were from 12 to 5pm each day.

I decided to go for the throat of Mrs. Houghton, together with the whatever of Dr. William Harvey.

#

A small somewhat stout woman, about fifty, with white hair tied up in a bun, with a firm suspicious smile, welcomed me into her consulting room -- which was little larger than a closet. There was a chart on the wall that listed her fees for various cures and medicines.

My phony pitch was that I suffered from neuralgia and that none of the usual tonics or pills seemed to help. Thus I had come to Dr. Harvey.

"I'm sorry Mr. Cumberland, but my control is not present this day. I cannot simply summon him as he has duties on the other side. I must await his pleasure." She looked me over, passing her hands around me as I sat in the medical chair. "These pills will help prepare you for Dr. Harvey, should you return tomorrow."

She placed three yellow pills from a larger jar into a small envelope, smiled her suspicious smile, and led me to her door. Though she didn't ask it, I paid her the 2s 6d fee according to her chart. She accepted the money without a smile.

Charles Stewart, a public analyst at 47, York Road, Lambeth, after about twenty minutes of testing, told me the pills were only sugar and of no medical benefit. He signed his name to that statement. Now all I needed was for Dr. Harvey to prescribe a cure, and I had Mrs. Houghton.

I was at her door at twelve the following day to finally meet the spirit of Dr. Harvey.

Mrs. Houghton positioned herself in her chair in front of me and bossed with one eye. She appeared to go into a trance, slumping back against the chair. After a moment or two, speaking in deep and gruff voice, she said, "Do you want to be overhauled?"

I said, "Yes."

She caught both of my hands, pronouncing in her gruff voice, "Your neuralgia is very bad, sir. You have a very nervous disposition … and you are suffering from a liver complaint as well." The Harvey voice paused. "And Mr. Cumberland, you suffer from a spinal ailment. You must place yourself in the hands of your medium, who will cure all of your ailments, if you follow her directions."

Houghton moved her hands about my face for about ten minutes, then snapped her fingers.

Harvey's gruff voice told me to ask the medium for direction, which I did.

"Take Pond's Extract and four of the blue pills," she said.

The medium put some Extract in my mouth, which I swallowed with some difficulty. Ah, the sacrifices that a gallant thought reader must make in the public's defense. She gave me a small bottle of the Extract with its greenish color and greenish fragrance.

Harvey remained in our presence long enough to wish me well, then departed to his minister to his more spiritual patients.

At the door, I paid Mrs. Houghton five shillings for the two medicines as stated on her chart and wished her a good day.

At Lambeth, after about half an hour, Stewart gave me a signed note stating that the blue pills were only sugar, and that the Extract could not impact my spine, my liver or my neuralgia. Even the American manufacturer claimed only that it would quickly settle an upset stomach, "and such-like troubles".

So, the best that the great William Harvey, who died three hundred years ago, could do was to prescribe sugar and an American stomach elixir.

I had her!

CHARGES AGAINST A SPIRITUALIST.

Miss Martha Ann Houghton, about 50 years of age, described as a healing clairvoyante, of Park-street, Grosvenor-square, has been charged at the Marlborough-street police-court, London, at the instance of Mr. Stuart Charles Cumberland, journalist and lecturer, with obtaining 2s. 6d. and 5s. from him by false pretences. Three other summonses charged her with having used "subtle craft, means, and devices by palmistry or otherwise, to deceive and impose on Stuart Charles Cumberland by pretending to hold communication with the spirit of a deceased person, to wit, Dr. Harvey, the discoverer of the circulation of the blood, contrary to the statute."

With the certainty of convicting Houghton printed on my handbills, I was able to book a lecture at Steinway Hall with an assured newspaper presence.

Using some of the tricks of Irving Bishop, together with a few of my own, with scalp in hand, though actually only at my fingertips, I was able to deliver a creditable lecture to match against Bishop and the magicians. I pocketed £7, and six mentions in the papers that I could find. *Brief: the Week's News,* page 333, provided the most wholehearted account.

SPIRITUALISM.—Mr. Stuart Cumberland, a gentleman who has become known by his recent exposure of a notorious spirit medium, lectured on this subject last Monday at the Steinway, Hall, Lower Seymour-street. He may fairly claim to have successfully exposed some of the tricks which have been indulged in by so-called spirit media and others. Having treated his audience to a veritable dark *séance*, as given by the professional spiritualists, he showed that the agency at work was the medium's hand, which had previously been released from the custody of the person sitting at his side by an operation whose ingenuity would enable the performer to escape detection in a darkened room. One of his tricks he described as a reproduction of the spiritualist Furman's manifestation of shooting at an entranced medium; but, as there is just a possibility in this trick of the medium being shot in earnest, we doubt whether it enjoys a wide popularity among spirit media.

I had noticed that no other exposer of mediums had ever presented an exposure of the Furman stunt, but when you are only at the second rung of the ladder, you must push the edge. Following the lecture and a few questioners, I did make two contacts with good future potential, so the entire endeavor was an unqualified success, i.e., until I walked into the Marlborough Street police-court the next day with Mr. Edward Pain, my solicitor.

#

I was sworn as Stuart Charles Cumberland, and Pain began his questioning, in which I detailed my Houghton experience. The Stewart notes were given as evidence. I paid £2 for his time, thus Stewart was in the audience to answer questions as necessary. At the end of almost two hours of detailed specifics, the magistrate adjourned the case to the next day, as a violent crime took priority for the balance of the day.

#

In reconvening the next day, the counsel for Mrs. Houghton, Mr. Samuel Abrahams, a tall, angular man of black hair down to his shoulders, asked the court to detail the charges he was to answer on behalf of his client. The magistrate did so. Abrahams sat down, smiling.

I was sworn again, and again I had paid Stewart £2 to be in the audience. Pain led me again through the Houghton experience. It was clear we had her. I expected Abrahams, with Houghton sitting meekly beside him, would simply negotiate an appropriate settlement with the court, and myself, the case would be closed and I could begin to print my new handbills.

Nodding to the magistrate, who looked unusually pale and had been coughing since court had opened, Abrahams said, firmly without any histrionics, "Nothing has been proven, sir, nothing. I do not doubt for a moment the analysis of Mr. Stewart of the items presented to him by Mr., ah, Cumberland. But nothing has confirmed that any of those items came from my client's hand, except the word of the plaintiff, under oath I recognize, but nevertheless without independent witness. Therefore the pills and extract mean nothing in this case. Neither has Mr., ah, Cumberland, proven that the presence of Dr. William Harvey was a fraud, as nothing has been proven one way or another regarding my client's spiritual guidance. There is, therefore, Mr. Magistrate, no case to adjudicate, and I ask for immediate dismissal of the case and that the prosecutor be required to pay my client a sum to compensate her for her time and discomfort." He sat down as the magistrate began coughing more heavily, and clearly needed medical help.

The magistrate struck his desk once with his gavel. "Until tomorrow at this time. Good morning," he managed.

As Pain and I walked by Abrahams and Houghton, he glanced up at me, and stage-whispered, "Is it Cumberland, sir, or Garner?

#

As we sipped our brews at the Bloody Two Squires pub, Pain very succinctly explained my position. "You have lost your case, Charley, and on cross-examination tomorrow, Abrahams will charge you with perjury because of swearing to Cumberland as your name. Magistrate Burney does not tolerant any lying in his court, so you will be find yourself facing a year or more in prison, possibly in chains, and a £100 fine." He finished his tankard and signaled for another.

I held my head in my hands. No scalp -- and not even any chickens, it seemed. There was no choice. I pushed my brew to one side. "We need to withdraw the charges. Can I do that?" I hadn't planned on Houghton having a competent solicitor. I should have taken someone with me as a witness, but just didn't think of it. I wanted the scalp to be all mine. I had assumed … No, I was just an ass." Another naïve … From Pain's expression, my face must have twisted in anger, stupid anger.

Pain nodded. "But we will get resistance from Abrahams. He knows, somehow, your East Oxford life and will have that all over the papers, *if he chooses*. Stuart C.

Cumberland will cease to exist, if we are lucky, and that is our only defeat."

#

Abrahams publicly refused at first to accept my withdrawal of charges "in solicitation for his client's health", but then after turning to his client, relented. Pain's paying him £25 for his client's whatever, had closed the deal the night before -- and had almost drained my Cumberland account.

Brief: the Week's News, unfortunately, as generous in my defeat as in my victory, printed, on page 391:

The Healing Clairvoyante.—At Marlborough-street Police-court last week the summonses against Miss Houghton, the so-called "healing clairvoyante," were withdrawn, on the application of Mr. Pain, solicitor for Stuart Cumberland, the prosecutor. Mr. Abrahams, for the defendant, stated that he was prepared to go on with the case, and declared that the real reason for the application was that the prosecutor wished to avoid cross-examination as to his antecedents. He also informed the magistrate that a summons would be taken out against Cumberland for perjury.

Several weeks later, I did defeat the popular materializing medium, Harry Bastian, in a highly spectacular manner that garnered several very rewarding stories, even including *Punch*, that provided that scalp, that credibility that I so needed. That, along with my maturing thought reading skills, finally moved the chickens out of sight. The Houghton experience had shaken me to the core, forced me to face the realities of what I was trying to do. Conning Victoria's realm with a manufactured persona, however carefully planned, had sharper edges than I had ever understood standing behind a butcher's countertop in East Oxford.

An expensive lesson -- but now I could plan for the world.

THE CHEVALIER --

FIRST CLASS

"What is called society loves to patronize, and, as a matter of course, hates to be patronized; and it goes without saying that such rarified society will never receive as an equal any man whom it can hire."

I wrote that squib several months back in my first book, *People I Have Read,* due out in London next month in an unfortunately cheap edition for three bob by Sampson Low & Marston publishers in time, they said, for Queen Victoria's 65th birthday celebration. My take from each cheap volume was ... unsatisfactory ... to be courteous.

Damn unsatisfactory to be more accurate. The publishers offered to buy my book outright for £50 which I refused. I want to own my material. Ah, well, I'll chalk it up to a potentially promising publicity opportunity. This urgent timing was dictated because the Good Lady and several of her closest minions are mentioned in my book; with some unique candor, which may attract the British public's attention.

My handbills and advertisements call me a thought reader; while some observers have called me a mind reader, some even a wizard, a necromancer -- some, naturally, call me a variety of lesser things, but that is of no matter. It only juices the public interest and bucks up my take.

Obviously, one who lays siege to the wealthy and the aristocratic classes of this Age requires a certain coolness of mind, a suitably euphonious name, a style of speech, dress and careful culture; along with a flutter-finger background that no one can quite pin down.

So, of course, I turned down the 10,000 French francs performance fee offered by the Princess Alexandra, precipitously late of Greece and its sometimes lethal political ills, and, bowing, accepted the engagement at her palatial villa outside Vienna as a gentlemanly honor to place myself at the service of Her Royal Highness.

Her Royal Highness's envoy's jaw dropped abruptly to a satisfying level, his eyes went round. After a moment, he recovered his aristocratic calm.

"Sir ... ah, Herr Cumberland," stammered Count Josef Marran, bowing slightly, his oiled black hair glistening in the gaslight of my hotel sitting room. Richly arrayed in Viennese court dress, complete with dark blue satin breeches, the small man with an Imperial goatee resembled a chocolate doll from a patisserie near the Stephansdom. "You will not accept ten thousand francs? Ah, yes, Her Highness will be most pleased ... and," he added quickly, "of course, be moved by such devotion from such a distinguished English gentleman and honored guest."

The Princess was pleased and would welcome me as her guest, as an equivalent to the titled toffs and generals -- not as a hired act to be dismissed to the kitchen once my wonders were concluded.

But then, according to the scurrilous rumors that circulate in those drinking establishments patronized by discriminating thought readers, Her Royal Highness could use the ready cash to help cover some pressing and embarrassing debts; which was why the financier and holder of most of the royal debts, Julius Oldenburg and his grimly suspicious wife, were the center of her attentions. That, after only the barest and briefest nod toward me as I entered the brilliantly lighted salon with four fireplaces blazing.

I, her gallant English guest and thought reader -- worked her stylish soirée for free -- but paid well in social confirmation.

Of necessity, my memories of the Oxford butcher shop, its sounds, sometimes slimy touch, along with its always unique aromas, always remain fresh.

#

An English ten-pound note had been sealed in an envelope and its serial number memorized by the hulking Grand Duke Michael of Russia while I was out of the salon. I was then blindfolded and led back to the bejeweled crowd by the charming Princess herself, her anxiety obvious from the tremors I detected in holding her delicate wrist at my fingertips.

My fiddle is that I read thoughts through my refined discernment and perception of such virtually imperceptible nervous vibrations. Such unconscious quivering is caused by the subject's concentration on a specific compelling topic; such as the location of a pin or other object which I then locate within seconds after being brought back into the room, though blindfolded and barely touching the subject's hand or forehead. But in the Princess's case, even an untrained observer could detect her intense concentration on dangerously overdue royal debts.

On occasion, I have pressed my thought reading capabilities to the limit of risk. Instead of actually touching the subject, I maintain contact with her only through a silk handkerchief, the ends of which are held by the subject and me. Consequently, I read the subject's thoughts *without* direct physical contact, which refutes the American physician George Miller Beard's assertion last year in New York newspapers that thought reading only amounted to 'muscle-reading', an ugly term that Beard coined; but which is awkwardly accurate in its insight. Mere muscle-reading is transformed into edgy, mystical thought reading through a serious showmanly presentation.

I held the Grand Duke's large sweaty liver-spotted hand flat against my forehead with my left hand as I began to move the pen above the white panel braced on a tripod. As I moved my right hand in a circular motion, I detected his hesitancy in resisting my completing the circle. I started another smaller circle, and experiencing resistance, I wrote a 3.

There was a gasp from the audience at the Duke's grunt of confirmation.

I continued in a like manner through the seven digits and in about forty seconds had written the serial number correctly that had been known and locked only in the mind of the Grand Duke.

"My God, sir," said the Grand Duke, stepping back to join in the restrained applause of the aristocratic assembly. "That was truly uncanny. How deep into the human mind can you go?"

"As deeply as my subject will allow me, Your Imperial Highness," I said. Which was true, but the thought reader can actually read only direction and location from the subject; and must interpret from those two inputs the number, object or design on which the subject is concentrating.

While blindfolded, with the Czar as subject, I have even written Russian words, though I know nothing of that language.

"And now, your Royal Highnesses, my Lords, ladies and gentlemen, I wish to arrange an assassination." The faces of several of the titled guests went pale, as they had in recent weeks been publicly marked by assassins in Russia, Greece and Bulgaria. "But only an imaginary assault, I assure you," I said, smiling and bowing.

The titled faces remained pallid.

Bearing a noble title in some parts of Europe in 1884 was akin to wearing a large target on your back.

Continuing, I explained, "After I have been escorted out of the room, and the door closed, please select an assassin from among your company, decide what weapon that person will use and where that weapon is hidden; and, who shall be the intended victim.

"I shall endeavor, on my return *and* blindfolded, and only through entering the mind of one who knows all the details of this imaginary crime, to identify the victim, the kind and location of the weapon ... and finally ... to place my hand on the assassin."

Finally, after about five minutes, I was led blindfolded back into the twittering glittering salon. I waited until someone touched one of my extended hands. Looking down the side of my nose under the blindfold, I could see the elegant dancing shoes of Prince Louis of Reuss-Schliez, the scion of an impoverished German principality long absorbed into the German Empire of the Iron Chancellor, the Prince Otto von Bismarck.

Louis was a young man, handsome, of slight stature, modest intelligence, artistic taste and a nervous manner; but who was, I had discovered in my researches in the last two days, an excellent horseman, impulsive gambler, and remarkably courageous.

He could not have been a worse selection as my mental guide. Louis had impressed me as someone who could not concentrate on anything for very long. But thought readers cannot always control their milieu.

It was also rumored that Prince Louis had lost his heart to the attractive Princess Alexandra, and that she had reciprocated.

"Ah, Prince Louis," I said. His hand started, as though I could not have guessed who he was. I smiled and suppressed a laugh. Ah, well, royal sir, I am a thought reader, after all. "First, concentrate on the victim, the target of this imaginary foul act." There was a modest gasp at my use of blunt words. All the better to help focus Louis' thoughts.

I had failed once earlier in the evening when the Dowager Duchess of Frederick failed to hold a thought long enough to be a successful subject and had to be, with some embarrassment, replaced by another noble lady to enable my wonder to be completed. I was now relying on the probability that Louis would not want to fail in front of his Princess.

Moving quickly, in only a few seconds, the tiny tremors in Louis' wrist led me cleanly -- to the brilliantly dressed in black and silver and spurred-boots, Count Heinrich Wagner, the notorious Chief of Police of Vienna.

"*Gut,* Herr Cumberland," growled the Count, "but finding a body is something any policeman can do."

I bowed. "Now," I said, "the weapon. What is it and where is it hidden?"

Again, Louis' intense concentration, and the unconscious tremors from his increasingly sweaty hand, silently led me to a bookcase. As I passed my free hand over the shelves I detected a distinct hesitation in Louis' manner, stopped. Then I let my hand pass over the contents of that shelf, but not touching anything. Again, a subtle hesitation -- time and position coalescing. I lowered my hand onto a small bronze statue in the shape of an attacking eagle. I held it up. The steady murmuring of the crowd jumped in volume.

With the audience confirmation, I declared, "An excellent plan, but now … now the assassin. The *fiend* himself." Again a sharp gasp. I laughed. "Please. This is only a play. Please don't be alarmed by my dramatizations."

But -- confound it! -- in my search for the assassin, I could not detect anything from Louis. This was the climatic finale, to seal my evening's performance, the final wonder.

I moved about the room, quickly at first, sweat beginning to trickle down my back from the four blazing fireplaces, banking on Louis' continued strong guidance, but, damnit, there was none. I stumbled at one point over a small table, upsetting someone's champagne glass; but still nothing. Moving more slowly a second time about the room gave the same blank result.

Returning to the center of the room, I dropped Louis' hand. I paused, my own hands becoming sweaty but not from the replenished fireplaces. Two choices. Prince Louis himself was the assassin or, he was, consciously, blanking his mind to protect the real assassin, his Princess Alexandra. To declare the Princess and be wrong could create an awkward social moment -- but to guess Louis and be wrong -- but neutralizing failure by using the proper phrasing. A thought reader, like any gambler, must recognize his odds and play accordingly.

"Ah, Prince Louis, your Highness, you are accepting the guilt of the assassin," I said, removing and tossing the blindfold away in a hopefully gallant manner.

Louis' immediate flush assured me that the guilty party was the Princess.

"As a gentleman, sir, you stoutly protect the precious reputation of ... our royal hostess." Turning, I bowed low to the Princess who, with a brilliant smile, rose from her chair and immediately began to applaud. She nodded to me. She was joined immediately by the rest of the audience, their medals and jewelry tinkling gently in the background.

#

That gentle sound was my first thought when, at three the next morning, I wearily opened my hotel room door to a frowning Count Heinrich Wagner with a helmeted, beribboned, and armed police officer stationed immediately behind him.

"Herr Cumberland, Herr Julius Oldenburg has been murdered," he said. "Stabbed in the heart." His expression changed to a snarl of anger. "Her Royal Highness has *insisted* that I call upon you to join the investigation. Your theatrics of last night have unfortunately convinced the inexperienced Princess that you are 'indispensable' to finding *this assassin*."

#

There is always a discreet social time for even distinguished guests to depart; which I had done a little over an hour after the close of my thought reading demonstration. Multiple conversations had enveloped me as I shifted about the salon, champagne in hand, providing my card to numerous requests for my services at other engagements; along with promises of additional introductions in other major European, North American and African cities. That hour more than offset any loss of performance fees. Before withdrawing from her guests, the Princess herself, with Prince Louis in tow, escorted me to my waiting carriage.

"My dear Mr. Cumberland," she had said, her gentle musical voice warming my inner butcher-shop soul, "you have enchanted us and my other guests in a manner that we will never forget. You are always welcome in our house."

The royal "we" had resonated perfectly with her blonde beauty and regal presence. I bowed over her extended hand, brushed it gently with my lips and departed.

An odd experience from an earlier time suddenly broke into my mind as the lighted villa was lost behind me in the trees. It had always been difficult in the past to inspire feminine interest with hands that had reeked of chicken guts.

#

But now her fresh blue eyes were red from tears, her delicate face torn with worry -- and terror. A killer had penetrated her royal hospitality, her most private sanctum. Embarrassment for any deep affront to an honored guest, yes, naturally, always.

But a killing?

Unthinkable.

None of her aristocratic society would risk entering her house again; until the assassin was found and his political affiliation identified. What country, what organization was the terrorist from? Was Oldenburg the intended target -- or had there been a mistake and it was really one of *them* the killer had sought? Oldenburg did bear a general physical resemblance to the burly Grand Duke Michael.

Oldenburg had been found with a knife in his chest, lying face-up in a snow-covered courtyard at the rear of the villa which overlooked a turbulent river, black with winter. The river's course delineated the boundaries of much of the Princess's estate. Her villa stood on a small peninsula that was shaped roughly as a wolf's head.

The first problem was that the body of the financier lay surrounded by unblemished snow and no footprints. There was no snow on Oldenburg's body. There had been no new snow since shortly before I had arrived for the evening's soirée when Oldenburg was still very much alive.

The body had been discovered by the Dowager Duchess of Frederick on her way to her second floor bedroom when she looked down from a window. Her screams had brought the servants, the Princess, Prince Louis, and finally Count Wagner, who had not yet left the villa.

I was immediately surrounded by the sleepy and frightened faces of the once haughty noble guests murmuring something about a "magic assassin" who could walk above the snow; who could kill without leaving any trace or sound.

Count Wagner had warned me of the atmosphere I would encounter. With Oldenburg's aggressive business practices, the police chief did not discount one of Oldenburg's clients from the city tracking him out to the villa.

"Cursed people bring blood with their money," Wagner had snarled as we drove up to the villa. "I, myself, only escaped his clutches two months ago. His demands for repayment on my son's financial indiscretions were intolerable.

"I understand several of the guests last night, as well as the Princess herself, are his clients."

As we climbed down from his carriage, he said, "There is no shortage of motive for killing someone as Herr Oldenburg … assuming he was the target … but, regardless, I must find this killer quickly.

"So, Herr Cumberland, you are here at the royal request, not mine. Stay away from my investigation."

#

"It is reassuring," Count Josef Marran murmured to me, as we followed Wagner and his troops down the hallway leading to the fatal courtyard, "is it not, Mr. Cumberland, that the police of Austria are of the proper class; not, as in your country, where the police populate their ranks from the lowest classes of laborers and laborers' sons."

The oiled ass left out butchers and butchers' sons.

Easily seen in the light from six torches placed around the courtyard, there were now footprints all over the snow, but the impression left in the snow by Oldenburg's body was almost untouched. He had been sprawled out on the ground, as if falling while trying to escape his attacker.

Oldenburg was a tall, obese man, whose leering smile would be difficult for any debtor to look at for long. I had avoided using him as a subject in my performance. He didn't feel right, as though he was eager to despoil whatever I was doing. But no assassin could have stabbed Oldenburg and then thrown his large body twenty feet out into the middle of the courtyard without using a siege engine. There was no snow on his body, only snow beneath his body.+

I don't believe in spirits or the supernatural, so how could this *Finanzmann* get stabbed surrounded by fresh snow without any footprints? Why the added mystery? Just killing would seem to be enough.

I looked up and around when we stepped through stout etched glass doors out into the courtyard. I had not removed my coat since arriving as the icy chill near the river had become even more penetrating.

The courtyard was enclosed within crenellated stone walls at least ten feet high that abutted against the stone and brick walls of the villa, which itself rose a further two floors above. The single large wooden gate in the courtyard was chained and barred from the inside and, Count Marran confided, was rarely used during the winter. There was an unbroken ice pack accumulated against the bottom of the gate.

A heavy green tile roof overhung the edge of the courtyard and sloped at one end out toward the tumultuous roaring river. An old watch tower was just visible above the crest of the roof on the river side, outlined by the light of a gibbous moon.

According to Count Marran, Oldenburg's wife had returned to the city shortly after my leaving, pleading an illness. The Count, ever alert in the Princess' cause, had overheard Oldenburg say something about a "royal client", who would drive him back into the city later.

Following my circuit of the courtyard, I began to feel multiple eyes on me, as though I could wave my hand and announce the killer and the means.

"May I view the remains, Count Wagner?" I asked. He nodded curtly and tossed his hand toward one of his men who led me to a back dining room.

The table looked as if was on the verge of collapse from Oldenburg's huge body. He must have weighed over seventeen stone. The knife, a nondescript blade similar to thousands used in the area, was plunged into the lender's chest but leaving almost three inches of metal showing. As a policeman pulled and twisted with both hands, finally wrenching the knife free, blood grouted out splattering over his uniform. Cursing savagely, the copper slammed the dagger on the table and stepped back.

I was surprised, but not at the actions of the policeman. The blade was much longer than I had expected. The killer had managed to drive the knife barely halfway into his victim, but, obviously, deep enough.

Some of the titled guests wrapped in richly embroidered silken robes had gathered at the dining room door, not daring to enter the room, anticipating something from me that the police would not do. I am a thought reader, so...

"Please stand away, officer," I said to one of Wagner's men who approached to pick up the dagger. "I need complete isolation of the decease's mind."

Still wiping at his bloody uniform, the policeman stepped back, a quizzical frown across his face.

I caught a glimpse of Wagner stopping to glance into the room as I placed my hands flat against Oldenburg's cool forehead. I closed my eyes. I frowned to suggest a difficult internal effort, a maximum mental process. A light greenish cast was forming across the dead man's bloating features. The varied fragrances of the financier were also gathering strength.

"What?" I heard the Princess hesitantly murmur behind me.

"I am striving, your Highness, to grasp, to detect the fading thoughts of Herr Oldenburg, to see if the killer's identity is still locked somewhere deep into his mind."

That's nonsense, of course, but it plays very well in the papers. And it did give me time to think. With the dead man's arms folded over his chest and his body rolled over on his right shoulder, I did see a small red paint smudge on the back of Oldenburg's suit coat near his right shoulder.

I couldn't recall seeing any red in the villa. The Princess seemed to be given more to gold, silver and blue in her interior design. But then he could have picked up the smudge anywhere, and everyone was too guarded in the man's dominating presence to have pointed out the smudge to him.

"My God, man!" said Grand Duke Michael. "Can that be possible?"

I didn't answer.

It was obvious that Julius Oldenburg was not attacked in the courtyard. Neither his nor the killer's footprints were in the snow. And there is no magic, even though the various guests were still muttering something about a wizard with a knife -- like something out of an exotic paperbound Shilling Shocker. So my first question was: where *was* he killed? The how might follow; then, finally, perhaps, the who.

Raising my hands, I shook my head as if to clear it of interference. I stepped back, nodded to the policeman. "The deceased is now yours, officer. His mind has faded to black."

Wagner had now stepped into the room and stood at the foot of the table.

"What insanity is this!" he exploded at me, his large blue eyes bulging.

"I have been seeking the last flickering images in Oldenburg's mind. He was not killed in the courtyard, my dear Count," I said, calmly, apparently indifferent to his rage. But Wagner could cause me serious trouble with only a snap of his fingers. "The victim was killed elsewhere and his body somehow transported to where it was found. There was still a blurred image fading rapidly in his mind that suggests he was killed by a man smaller in stature than he was."

That, naturally, was obvious from the location of the knife wound and the fact that Oldenburg was taller than anyone, other than the Grand Duke, at the reception.

The titled on-lookers murmured at these inspired revelations; fear was vivid across their faces.

"And, it would appear, sir," I said bowing toward the angry police chief, "it would appear that the killer is still within this villa." An unchallengeable guess -- but one that *could* be true.

That brought a sharp gasp from everyone. Her hands to her pale face, the Princess whispered, "Still here? To kill again? You must protect us, Count Wagner, with however many men are necessary."

Wagner struggled to rein in his annoyance toward me as he turned to the stricken Princess. "I will have an armed guard at the door of every bedroom within the next five minutes, Your Royal Highness." He started from the room, first throwing me a murderous glance.

Well, I was in the pot for sure now. I was committed to exercise my mystic skills to track down this wizard with a knife. Preferably before the police did their workmanlike job. All I had said, Wagner certainly already understood. My theatrics had gained me an implacable enemy; true, but also, *potentially*, a hurricane of publicity.

#

Count Marran led me to the window from which the Dowager Duchess had first seen the body. The impressed image of the dead man was still visible below, but it was slowly filling with a new light snow fall. The body image was off-center, something not obvious when standing next to it on the ground. It lay closer to this wing of the villa.

As angrily demanded by Count Wagner, I was staying well clear of the police chief and his uniforms. I have had one or two run-ins with British constables and, upper class or lower, I try to stay clear of any police.

We continued to walk to the end of the hall which overlooked the river below, virtually invisible in the night except for its sustained roar. The watchtower stood hardly fifteen feet away. It was wooden, not stone like the rest of the villa.

"The Princess insists that the tower be maintained as her grandfather had in the past. Bands of Slavic brigands would ride down from those hills and be on the villa before anyone could raise an alarm. Thus," Count Marran said, gracefully tossing his hand toward the watchtower, "that tower was built. The raids were stopped."

"The watchers would freeze to death on a night like tonight, would they not?" I said. "Loyalty and devotion are admirable, my dear Count, but there must be some practicality."

He laughed and pointed to a small door set into the wall. "You are quite right, Herr Cumberland. There is the inside watchtower used during the worst weather. Come."

The room was finished yellow stone, walls and ceiling, about eight feet long, four feet wide with a black curtain pulled back against one wall. The one large window bowed out toward the watchtower, so that someone standing in the bow could observe the far corners of the villa. As the Count explained, the black curtain was drawn behind the duty watcher so that any lights in the room would not distract him.

The window was ice cold when I touched it. Even in the moonlight, the far corners of the villa were easily visible. As I turned I saw that the window sill was painted red.

Count Marran answered my question. "The Princess' grandfather wanted the watchtower to be outlined in red to facilitate sighting on it when hunting or chasing the robber bands."

I stood back from the window. Oldenburg's head could have almost touched the ceiling here. But the confining walls would have prevented him from using his apparent strength effectively against a sudden attack of a wizard with a knife.

With a knife in his heart, Oldenburg would have become simply an ungainly lead weight as the killer struggled mightily to raise up, then push the body across the window-sill onto the roof, and then with a final shove, down the roof into the river below.

I shook my head. Royal blood tends to run thin after only a generation or two. That probably also applies to their luck.

With the candle that Count Marran had brought, I examined the floor near the window and found two small drops of partially dried blood -- and the killer's mark. Now, my issue was to announce the killer before Wagner and his uniforms performed the same work I had done. I could already hear him issuing orders in the distance.

#

With Wagner's icy forbearance, I asked the Princess and her guests to reassemble, dressed as the night before, in the salon. There were armed officers at each of the six salon doors. Servants were actively rebuilding blazes at two of the fireplaces.

The gowns were wrinkled, the colorful uniforms hastily buttoned and the sashes and sparkling bejeweled orders off-centered. There was only one order that I wanted to see, but I needed to have all of them displayed to ensure the killer would not anticipate me.

"Thank you, Your Royal Highness, my Lords, ladies and gentlemen, for accommodating me at this difficult hour and great inconvenience."

"Is the killer here, Herr Cumberland?" immediately asked Grand Duke Michael, his fists like bricks.

When I nodded, a sharp gasp escaped the gathered nobility. They frantically looked about them like deer in a trap.

"There is here in this room an object, an object tied to the killer, of which perhaps even he, for it is a man, is not aware.

"I am going to take each of the men by the wrist, as we did only a few hours ago, for just a moment. The killer will tell me who he is … he cannot conceal it from me … the killing dominates his mind, his thoughts. Thoughts," I bowed for emphasis, "that *I will read.*"

While blindfolded, I led each of the men for a few steps then moved to the next. I could see all I needed from under the blindfold down the side of my nose, but a bit of extra theatre could only enhance my reputation as a thought reader to be reckoned with.

I stepped back to the center of the room. Removing the blindfold, I threw it aside with a practiced cavalier toss of my hand. I bowed to the Princess and then to Prince Louis of Reuss-Schliez.

"As only a few hours ago, Prince Louis, you have again taken the responsibility for protecting the reputation of our royal hostess. You killed Julius Oldenburg to stop his demands on the Princess for payments. And, with better luck, you might have succeeded."

The rustling aristocrats quickly put space between themselves and Prince Louis, as he looked around at the guards at each door, then at his beloved Princess, her face frozen in shock.

It was sad. Both of them so royal, both in love; and both as broke as a butcher shop clerk on Monday.

Wagner stepped to Louis' side. He carefully noted the large multi-beamed silver order pinned to the gold and white sash across Louis' chest. He nodded. Then looked back at me and nodded again. He had confirmed the source of the diamond I had found on the lookout room floor.

"You are under arrest, Your Highness," said the police chief, "for the murder of Julius Oldenburg." He beckoned to two of the guards.

The Princess burst into tears. Two of the older ladies rushed forward to wrap their arms around her heaving shoulders.

"I did it for you, Alexandra! I couldn't bear that fiend's base attitude toward you," Prince Louis pleaded, looking back over his shoulder between the two policemen. "I did it to preserve your honor!"

"Honor!" she cried out, her voice breaking. "Honor? Honored *by murder*? That is outrageous. Honor is the payment of my debts, sir; not the butchery of the lender."

A telling point indeed.

Louis had lured Julius Oldenburg up to the lookout room with a promise of more business, then stabbed him. In Louis' struggle to raise and push the great body out the window, a diamond from one of the many orders pinned to the gold and white sash across his chest, had been pulled loose and fallen near the window.

A final push and Louis slid the body down the roof to fall, he had planned, into the black river. The body would not reappear, if it ever did, until miles downriver and days in the future.

But Louis' luck did not hold. With little control, once sliding freely, the body caromed off the red-painted watch tower and slid, instead, to drop down thirty feet into the courtyard onto the virgin snow. If the body had slid on the roof just two feet the other way, Prince Louis would now likely be a free and happy man; instead of the likely suicide that his royal class demanded.

But royal blood and luck often run thin.

With some reluctance, Count Heinrich Wagner had privately conceded that in my finding the blood spots and the lost diamond that I had gotten to the quarry first, but that was as far as it went. In the end, my hurricane of publicity amounted to little more than a soft summer zephyr; just a brief comment to reporters acknowledging "Herr Cumberland's slight aid to the official investigation".

#

As I stepped up into my railway carriage to meet my engagements in Munich, Count Josef Marran, still in court dress, pressed something into my hand. "A special gift, sir, from Her Royal Highness, in acknowledgement of your kind discretion, marvelous powers, and loyalty to her royal house."

Wrapped in a white silk pouch embroidered with the Greek royal coat of arms, it was a sparkling decoration worked in the shape of a multi-beamed six-pointed star -- but, given the condition of the royal purse, made only of silver-plated pewter with inlaid colored crystals. A blue and silver sash was folded in the pouch as well.

"You, Herr Cumberland, have been elevated by Her Royal Highness," the Count bowed low, "to the rank of Chevalier of the Order of the Silver Swan." He smiled. "First Class," he added, with yet a lower bow.

#

My tale finished, I raised my half-filled tankard to the five chaps around the table and leaned back in my chair.

"So, gentlemen, remember, the next time you expect me to pick up the tab at the Bloody Two Squires pub, that Chevaliers, particularly of the *First Class,* are to receive honor, not the bill."

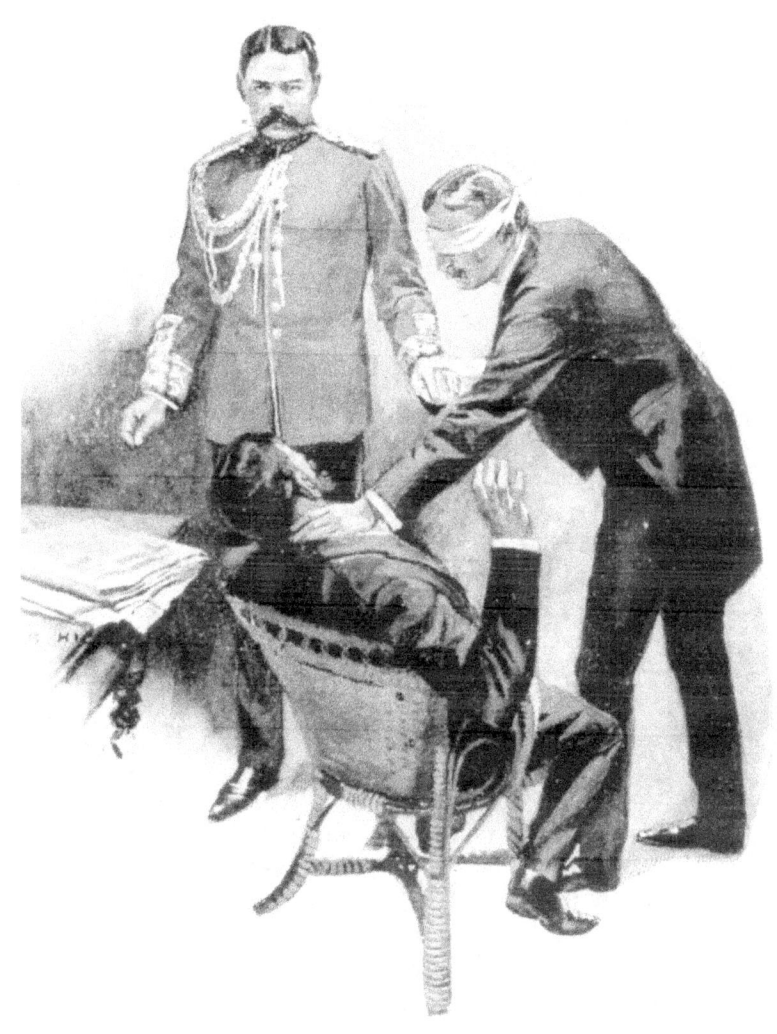

STUART CUMBERLAND

PERFORMING THE ASSASSINATION SCENARIO

WITH LORD KITCHENER

The Thief of Judpaw

"Mr. Stuart Cumberland," she said, in a voice so gently musical that it sounded more angelic than human. "You are a thought reader, and a very good one, as my uncle who lives in London has written me. Yours is a genuine talent, I know, because my sister and I have done some of the things you do in your soirees ... but not with your verve and style." She gathered her richly colored pink and purple sari and robe closely about her.

Shrimati Sarladevi was a female sorcerer -- at least that was how she had been described to me by Vicar Reginald Marley, a churchman of the Dissenter variety, but formerly a well-respected Anglican scholar. The Vicar had come out to India to live the rest of his life "away from the heavy screed of Westminster", as he had explained it, with a bit of an edge to his voice.

Marley had assured me that Sarladevi would be worth my time -- a lot of my time -- with some vague mutterings about genuine unanswerable powers. She was of a village, Judpaw, somewhere north of Bombay at the edge of the Punjab.

I smiled and nodded to her rich compliment. My first tour of India had commenced last night at the Bombay Town Hall. With excellent results, I might add, as Baron Reay, the Governor of Bombay, with his full bemedaled and uniformed entourage, was in attendance along with reporters from all the Bombay newspapers. A few prominent Indian merchants with their wives were also present -- but silently so.

My tour, arranged by Messrs. Rose & Co. through their Calcutta offices, would continue for about three months with most performances at the Station Clubs in the various military cantonments throughout northern India including a week, possibly two, at the viceregal villas in

Simla, finally concluding with a week at the Great Eastern Hotel in Calcutta.

There was little to gain performing for the natives, as I spoke none of their complex languages, and trying to perform thought reading through interpreters was near hopeless.

And, frankly, there was no money to be had in native venues.

The weather on the western Indian coast was growing muggy with temperatures approaching 90° F in the shade and would only get hotter in the days ahead; punctuated by occasional steaming rain showers, one of which had just started assaulting the roof of my hotel, the Ashok Imperial.

"But," Shrimati continued, still smiling her dazzling smile of perfect white teeth against her polished olive skin, her dark eyes fiercely alive, "there is a thought reading that lies beyond even your skills, sir."

"No doubt," I said, sipping my tea, a rich unforgettable Darjeeling, "this is India, after all, the land of mystery with three hundred languages, and a hundred religions with thousands of deities."

She laughed with a toss of her hand. "Only English fairy tales, written by travelers who never left their hotels or clubs." She smiled. "But you are right about the religions and the gods. We have more than enough of those."

Fairy tales?

Well, yes. I had embarked on the tour partially to be able to claim in my future advertisements back in Great Britain and the Continent that I had climbed the mysterious cloud-shrouded Himalayas to commune with hooded lamas who revealed their subtle faculties in shadowed temples that lay in secret valleys. As a courageous adventuring thought reader, an explorer of strange powers, I would gain greater public credibility with enigmatic India prominently displayed in my performing satchel -- and on my handbills.

I frankly doubted I would ever see a lama, hooded or otherwise, but no matter. It is the perceived message that draws the audiences, fills the seats. Rupees or pounds sterling -- it counted the same in the end, so long as there was enough of it.

"So," Shrimati said, rising, brushing back wisps of her black hair that momentarily fallen concealing her tika, the red mark on her forehead, "you will come? The Vicar, ah, he is not considered a correct Christian in your great English temples? Mr. Marley had said that you wanted to observe native magicians at their work."

I am not qualified to discuss the twistings of British Christianity, thus I simply confirmed the time and place as I held the door for her to float through. There was an aroma of mystery about this lady like nothing I had ever encountered anywhere in Europe -- spices I could not yet name.

As I closed the door, an odd thought occurred to me. Why had Marley described Shrimati Sarladevi as a "female sorcerer"? Why not just sorceress?

#

I read thoughts by detecting, while blindfolded, the almost imperceptible unconscious nervous tremors of a subject while touching or holding their hand or wrist as they concentrate upon a hidden object or other secret action; a talent I discovered to my very good fortune about three years ago.

For various reasons, not everyone in an audience is a good subject, a circumstance which can interfere with the pace of a performance, but there are those subjects who stand out, who make things easy.

A year ago, I was in the midst of a successful soiree in the main hall at the Glendevon Hotel in Bournemouth on the South coast of England. My subject was a delicate young Countess whose tremors I could easily read; but when she stumbled over the edge of a rug, her wrist slipped from my fingers. Yet .-- yet I could still sense her tremors even though, as I peeked down the side of my nose under my blindfold, her hand had fallen at least five or six inches from mine! I was still sensing her thoughts, her concentration -- without physical contact! I continued the demonstration without touching her with remarkable success. The applauding audience was unaware of what had happened; but I was shaken to the core.

I had no explanation for the phenomenon.

Since that pivotal night, I have found that of good subjects, of men perhaps one in fifteen I can read without contact; while with women it is closer to one in twenty. But I cannot *make it* happen. The sense is sometimes *just there*.

But the man I was now observing with Shrimati at my side and sweat trickling down my backside from the intense Indian sun, appeared to be reading thoughts at a distance of more than five feet. In fact, distance did not appear to be a factor for him.

The swarming native crowd that surrounded him at the edge of the village with its random collection of mud and stone huts was an amazing pallet of color and culture. Sword bearing Sikhs and Pathans, black clad Rajputs, Afghan traders stopping their camels for a moment, Mohammadans and Hindoos -- and, I think, one or two native Christians. The surrounding peepul, teak and bulky banyan trees were alive with raucous mynah birds chiding the jostling humans below.

A frowning black-suited British missionary with black-framed eye-glasses was at the far edge of the crowd, his small red scripture clutched tightly against his chest, the alien peoples shifting indifferently around him.

And, unlike the two-dimensional aspect of my thought reading, locality and direction being all that I can reliably sense; the tall golden-robed man was picking up unspoken details not possible for me, certainly not in this strange kaleidoscopic society. Shrimati's quietly whispered translations kept me abreast of the man's work.

He was not a Hindoo *faqir,* too tall and too clean, or even a *jogee,* a street magician of undetermined caste; but a lean hawk-visaged Afghan wearing a pointed green turban and a long ivory handled knife thrust in his waistband.

In our slow horse-drawn tonga ride from the train station, we had passed street stalls that displayed fly-covered skinned sheep carcasses and scrawny unplucked chickens hanging across their open shop fronts. The stalls reminded me of the back of John Weblin's butcher shop on St. Giles Street in Oxford, where, as just Charley Garner, I had worked as a clerk three years ago, but minus most of the flies.

Thought reading had liberated me from the chicken guts.

As we leisurely passed along the dusty roads in the tonga toward the village of Chandvad, I had seen several street magicians at work for English travelers near the train station. For all their mythic reputations, the Hindoo sleight-of-hand, even in passing, was crude, not up to the level that anyone could see for a few pence at any English music hall, or at Maskelyne's Egyptian Hall in Piccadilly.

The exotic motif in the street, however, with the cows wandering by, certainly would wash away any western stage setting, as would the varied odors and merciless heat.

"Magush," Shrimati explained to my question. "That is *pushto* for sorcerer, but not just a magician, only a man of tricks. A magush," she whispered, "can draw innocents to strange idols."

When I had commented earlier to Shrimati on my assessment of the manual skills of the Hindoo street magicians, she had only laughed. "I quite agree, Mr. Cumberland. Their magic is ... clumsy. Is that your word? That is why we travel away from the trains and the English travelers with their shiny copper coins."

As the magush turned toward the missionary, I noted that he carefully nudged the accumulated coins thrown at his feet under a folded robe behind him. The crowd opened before the extended hand of the magush like the waves before Moses, leaving the missionary isolated. All eyes were on the clearly labeled Christian.

In barely accented English, the magush said, "Good sah, please open your holy book to any page and focus your mind, your soul on a single verse thereon. Allow me, Haseeb Nabi, the privilege … the honor to read the gracious words of your book … only through your mind."

Glancing about him, at the men and women shuffling back from him, the missionary stepped back before the magush's extended hand and narrow smile.

"I wish you no harm, sah. As a man of God you know of these powers as written in your book. I mean only to ask this of you so that the English thought-reader standing behind me may be assured of the honesty of what I do."

I started and looked down at Shrimati who was laughing softly.

"The magush read your thoughts, Mr. Cumberland. Thought readers do have thoughts of their own … do they not?"

A few, yes, like, what the hell is going on here?

The missionary began to slowly thumb through his small red-bound Bible and then stopped somewhere near the center. His eyes behind his round black-framed glasses were afraid. No thought reading necessary to see that.

He was seriously afraid.

The magush took a step backward, then another. He looked over at me, and then very deliberately took another large step back, as though throwing down a challenge to me.

The missionary looked up, directly at Haseeb Nabi, straightened his shoulders. "I have a verse, sir," he said, his voice strained and high-pitched. He looked over at me, then back at the magush.

The crowd went silent. Even the camels, it seemed, stopped chewing.

In his strange pure English, Haseeb Nabi began. "Sah, your book says: He answered me then and said ... Measure, ah," he paused. "Measure thou the time diligently in itself; and ... when thou seest part of the signs past, which I have told thee before.

"It is a verse from your book called Second Esdras, is it not, sah? From chapter nine?"

The missionary went deathly pale. There was no doubt the magush had nailed his thought exactly, to the smallest detail. Squeezing his Bible, the churchman hesitated, then said, "Yes, Mr. Nabi, you are correct in every respect. A most impressive demonstration of Satan's powers, sir." He crossed himself and hurriedly walked away into the crowd.

Haseeb Nabi turned toward me. At the edge of my eye, I caught Shrimati's slight shake of her head. He bowed low to her, gathered up his robe and the coins from the ground and disappeared into the crowds.

"Come, Mr. Cumberland," said Shrimati, drawing a fold of the silken sari across her face, which left only her dark eyes revealed, "it is time for cool refreshment, is it not?"

Those, like me, who perform pseudo-miracles are the most frightened when confronted with the real thing -- because we, I, *know* it can't be done.

But it was.

I followed Shrimati's floating black and scarlet wrapped silken form toward the shade of a tented stall that stood away from the road. Large thick shiny green leaves grew over and about the tent like a giant hand reflecting the sun.

The crowds had now regained life. The camels were chewing again and the traders had resumed their loud declamations. It was as though the magush had never been there.

Edward Whinfield's familiar lines, translated from the work of the Persian mathematician and astronomer, Omar Khayyam, swept through my mind:

You ask what is this life so frail, so vain

'Tis long to tell, yet I will make it plain;

'Tis but a breath blown from those vasty deeps,

And then blown back to those same deeps again!

The vasty deeps, indeed.

The rich mango juice and crushed ice slid down my throat like a blessing direct from Heaven itself. After a quick glance at Shrimati, the serving wallah had waved away my payment.

I was about to ask how she knew the magush, when Haseeb Nabi suddenly appeared out of the ether at our little table. Maskelyne with his stage traps and mirrors at Egyptian Hall couldn't have conjured a more stunning appearance.

"So good to meet you, Mr. Stuart Charles Francis Cumberland," he said in his strange English, as he accepted a bowl of the mango and ice -- again without payment.

In close, his face was deeply lined, the weathered bronze skin stretched across high cheekbones, his sunken narrow dark eyes shadowed under thick brows flecked with silver. His slender high-bridged nose cast his face like that of a hawk, an alert predator.

His age was beyond my measuring.

"Your demonstration was impressive, Haseeb Nabi," I said. "I have not seen its like in Great Britain or Europe."

"You do me great honor, sah, by addressing me properly; and by your professional compliment. I am often amazed at the Christian missionaries, as Mr. James a few moments ago." He held up his hand. "I mean no disrespect to your Christ, Mr. Cumberland, but your missionaries remain remarkably ignorant of our cultures as they try to scare us away from our lands' gods with threats of hell and fire if we do not accept what they claim.

"Our own gods have their own fire and hells for us who stray from them. So," he laughed, "we will all burn, one way or another, it seems."

As we laughed at our shared fate, the magush drank his ice and mango.

"Mr. Cumberland," said Shrimati, "Mr. James has been a missionary for almost two years in this trading area, yet he rarely travels beyond this village. He does not speak any of the local languages. He relies on an interpreter from a lowly caste of street sweepers as his voice, so no one listens or makes note of him. He seems unaware that to address my friend as Mr. Nabi is an ignorant insult.

"I am sure Mr. James is a good man and, like all European missionaries we encounter, wants to deliver all of us benighted … is that the word? … natives to his heaven; but we have our own richly furnished heavens." She paused to glance quickly about her, then shrugged and said, "The English are too young a people to understand the gods of India ... Mr. Cumberland.

"Mr. James and his terribly worn wife will surely die of the heat here ... and the emptiness of their work."

The magush nodded. "If not of something else." His voice had dropped to a low growl that erased the spell of laughter of only a minute before.

"You travel on to the forest station, honored lady?" Haseeb Nabi asked.

Shrimati nodded. "It will provide Mr. Cumberland with a cool evening with the young officer there. We will continue on to Judpaw in the morning after his *chota-hazri*. Then we return to allow Mr. Cumberland to meet his performance schedule before the court of the raja of Jalia -- and the raja's *English minders*." She was not smiling.

We all rose as Haseeb Nabi bowed first to Shrimati, then extended his long-fingered hand to me. His grip was gentle, his manner less restrained.

"I return to my home in Qandahar beyond the Khyber Pass in a few days, Mr. Cumberland," he said. "I regret that I will not have the honor of experiencing one of your performances. I am sure ... as one professional to another ... that I would have much to learn from observing you."

Shrimati acknowledged his bow with whispered words in a language I could not understand. When I looked back, the magush had vanished.

#

The tonga ride toward the hills, the temperature dropping a few degrees as we climbed upward, was extraordinarily pleasant. The sharp metallic cries of the soaring broad winged kites overhead, the constant rustling of the jungle in the hot clean air, Shrimati's musical voice describing the birds and occasional flashes of deer punctuated by the sawing cough and sudden appearance of a panther. Long tailed grey langur monkeys chattered and shrieked above us then disappeared into the dense leaves.

The over-powering beauty, as the distant azure mountains, the famed Hindu-Kush, the distant pillars of the world, a part of the fabled Himalayas came into view just above the horizon.

Shrimati stiffened. "There, Mr. Cumberland! There! See him, next to that peepul tree with the broken limb." She ordered the tonga stopped. Shrimati's face was alive with excitement. "There! It is the spirit of the Lord Shiva. It is the Great Nag!"

She was out of the cart in an instant while I was still climbing down. I still couldn't see -- then, then I saw it as the hamadryad rose up above the brush.

Good God!

As I came closer, only about ten feet away, the serpent continued to raise its huge head until the cobra was looking me directly in the eye, its white hood spread, its forked tongue flicking in and out, shifting toward Shrimati, then as I moved, back toward me. Its hisses sounded like the growl of a large dog.

Shrimati continued to move closer, so I couldn't hang back. A butcher shop clerk would have the sense to run like hell the other way; but a gentleman, ah, a gentleman must never desert a woman in distress. But it appeared I was the one in distress. Social class consciousness could prove fatal in this case.

The big cobra suddenly moved toward her, ignoring me, then -- good God! *Another one!* A little smaller, the serpent rose up above the bush swaying as it appeared to pick its target -- me!

Her beautiful face flushed, Shrimati was ecstatic. "The two, a great omen sent us by the Lord Shiva! I have never seen a pair of what you English call king cobras together. The male, the Great Nag, can kill an elephant with a single bite!"

That statement began to reignite the sensible butcher shop clerk in me. But the snakes, their hoods spread, the scales of their heads reflecting the low sun shifted color from green to black to brown to yellow, as they rose still further up above the bushes like swaying white spirits, continued to shift always keeping the two of us centered in their cold black unblinking eyes. Then, suddenly, the big male lowered himself, his mate following, and they disappeared into the jungle.

Even in the growing coolness of the hills, I was sweating.

But, now I had a story that even the London *Times* would feature. And I had at least glimpsed the legendary

Himalayas -- and a magush, an Afghan sorcerer of undefined powers. My handbills could read like something out of the Arabian Nights.

And as we returned to the tonga, Shrimati still glowing from her encounter with Shiva, and I still sweating from my encounter with sheer terror, a thought suddenly intruded:

I felt I had not seen the last of Haseeb Nabi.

#

The forest officer, a subaltern, John Smythe-Howell, greeted me firmly by the hand. Fair haired, pale blue eyes, fair skin, he bowed as Shrimati waved to us from the tonga and disappeared down the hill. She would return for me after morning tea and breakfast.

Even with murderous temperatures in the shade during the day with wilting humidity, my youthful host came to our Spartan dinner in rigidly correct evening military attire. A stiff white iron-clad shirt, black tie, with appalling starched cuffs, a still more awful high collar that scraped with every movement, and a heavy gold trimmed close-fitting green jacket.

I was still in my sweat-stiffened cotton shirt and traveling suit, and I had loosened my tie. I had only a single change of shirt with me. Everything else was back at my Bombay hotel.

His face reddened with the heat, Smythe-Howell explained to my raised eyebrows. "Though I rarely have guests, or even see another Englishman except on quarterly inspections, I always dress because it keeps me in touch with the old home, and it keeps me from going slack." He felt that was the sublime secret of the Raj, of the Englishman in India -- that thing about "never going slack". Of impressing the natives with the innate discipline of the British caste; even if most of the Englishman, like the missionary James, couldn't speak the languages or touch the culture, rarely leaving their military cantonments.

Smythe-Howell's devotion to Queen and Empire was admirable to my English soul, but I wasn't sure that the natives saw that wearing impractical clothing and eating too much in the heat was evidence of a superior culture.

Behind their cultured politeness, the Indian populace likely had other thoughts.

When Smythe-Howell inquired about my travels, I mentioned my complex encounter with Lord Kitchener, a few months back in London, to which he raised some questions, the answers to which are more suitable to relate at another time.

My host nodded with intense interest at my tense description of the pair of king cobras.

"You were fortunate, Mr. Cumberland, that the snakes didn't feel threatened by you and Miss Sarladevi. In the jungle, they can move almost as fast as a man can run, and I've seen a pair of king cobras hunt in tandem, actually setting ambushes for their prey. They eat pythons, you know."

He sipped his port. "From your description, the male was probably about eighteen feet long. They can raise their heads up to about a third of their length. You were very fortunate to see the snakes at all. They were probably rubbing against the tree to help shed their skins. It is their season, you know, a time when they are easily irritated. Otherwise, they are very shy creatures and stay in the depths of the jungle.

"And your beautiful companion was right," he said. "One bite of a mature male king cobra can kill an elephant if the serpent can bite it on the trunk. It takes about three hours for the venom to do the job. I've seen that happen twice. It shakes the soul, sir, to experience that moment when the majestic elephant finally crumbles to the earth in death.

"There is," he added, smiling, "enough poison in one king cobra bite to kill twenty men."

As we rose to repair to bed, he said, "But as dangerous as they are, the Great Nag are beautiful creatures of God." He touched my arm. "By the way, Mr. Cumberland, there is a spectacled cobra that lives under this bungalow that keeps rats in check. He is generally active in the morning. Sleep well."

\#

A large village on the edge of a lake with a railway station only a mile away, Judpaw rumbled with activity, a market day, and Haseeb Nabi in the central square shaking his long flashing knife in the sun.

"We are like these thousands of grains of rice." He scooped a handful of rice from the great glistening crystal lotah bowl before him and threw it up to the winds that dispersed the grains across the crowd. "We are nothing, powerless."

The shimmering globular bowl bulged out like a turnip about two feet in diameter, then came back to a narrow neck that flared out into a wide flange around the center. It was the color of pure water. Some markings had been engraved into the flange, but I couldn't make them out.

Shrimati whispered, as she translated, that it was a holy bowl brought from the temple of Shiva a few miles away. It had been carved from a single block of rock crystal generations in the past, with the artist directed by Shiva himself in the form of an avatar, a wandering archer.

"Who would fear a people blown about like the rice? Who would care?" The magush's voice grew in anger and authority. "But," he turned in a circle, his right hand holding his knife, his left hand extended, pointing to each one, even to me. "But, bound together we have power, power from the Destroyer of Evil, from the Lord Shiva himself. Shrimati Sarladevi, his female sorcerer, has told you of the omens of the Great Nag." He suddenly shouted. *"Our omens!"*

His lean face was fierce, blazing with anger. "But there is power! Power from the Lord Shiva himself. To throw against the evil oppressor ... against those whose laws oppress us, ridicule us ... debase our religion with a pale Messiah. Power to bring back *our* Empire! Here is the Power, bound by the hands of Shiva himself."

The crowds were screaming their agreement, screaming against the British. I glanced around. I was the only Englishman in the square and probably in the village.

"Be not afraid, my friend. I am beside you," whispered Shrimati. "Watch!"

Haseeb Nabi had driven the crowds to a fierce frenzy. All trading had stopped. Even the passing Afghan traders had stopped to shout and shake their fists.

"Here is the Power! Behold the Power!" Haseeb Nabi raised his knife and plunged it into the packed rice in the bowl. He raised his knife again and plunged it once more into the rice. "Now!" he screamed, and drove the knife again deep into the rice. Then with both hands gripping the ivory hilt, his body crouched low, his shoulders straining, Haseeb Nabi raised the great bowl from the ground! Somehow, the knife, the rice and the bowl had become one!

Good God! What was this?

I heard Shrimati's voice raised with the crowd's as they cursed the British. All eyes were turning toward me. Scattered yells of *firinghi* and *goonda* and other shouts that sounded like choice Imperial insults rose in volume. Some men were shaking their fists at me.

I felt Shrimati's hand on my arm.

"Come. Now," she said. "Haseeb Nabi and I may not be able to restrain them much longer."

The sound faded to only a murmur when she closed the door of the warehouse shed behind us.

"What is going on, Shrimati?" I said. "I'm no expert on Imperial policies, but wasn't the Indian Congress Party just formed in Bombay with the approval of the Viceroy, Lord Dufferin, only a short time ago? With its explicit objective of leading India to ultimate independence?" I pointed toward the door. "What was that all about, out there?"

As if by my command, the door flew open and immediately closed. Breathing heavily, Haseeb Nabi stood before me. "Now, Mr. Cumberland," he said, "you have seen the Power of Shiva. What will you do?"

Shrimati answered me, her face cold. "The Congress Party is an effort of the British Raj to put us to sleep. To undermine the real independence movement, the real will of the people. Good people have been drawn to lead the Party, but they do not lead us, they do not lead the people! They are Victoria's lackeys!" Her voice crawled with contempt.

There was a sudden sharp bark and Haseeb Nabi crumpled to the wooden floor, a hole in his forehead.

I pulled Shrimati to the floor with me behind a wooden crate. "Stay here," I said and moved on my hands and knees to the edge of the crate. An open window, open knotholes in the planking in the back wall. A dozen places for someone to shoot through. I rose and jumped toward a side door, lowered my shoulder and broke it off its hinges.

In a few seconds, I was at the rear of the warehouse. No one was in sight. No footprints. No spent shell, so a revolver was used, not a repeater. Behind the shed there was open ground to low forested hills about fifty yards away. The killer clearly didn't go that way. He escaped into the still boisterous crowds in the square.

I turned to find Shrimati beside me.

"The killer has joined the crowd in front. Can you hold them, Shrimati? Hold the people in place to give me a chance to find the killer?"

Nodding, she ran to the front. I could hear her voice raised, telling of Haseeb Nabi's murder and that the killer was with them. No one was to be allowed to leave the square. Shiva's vengeance would be swift.

Maybe.

Great shouts of rage echoed around the square when I appeared. The omen of Shiva -- the killing of Haseeb Nabi?

"Tell them to line up," I said, "all but the children and women. In two rows ... there, and there." I carried the magush's long ivory-handled knife in my hand. "Tell them,

Shrimati, tell them that this knife, the Blade of Shiva, will mark the killer of Haseeb Nabi."

The surly crowd shuffled around, growing silent, but formed two straggling rows. Angry dark eyes surrounded me.

I didn't understand why I was in the middle of all this, but thought readers are drawn like magnets into strange affairs. And a remarkable man whom I had wanted to know better had been murdered in front of me, for whatever reason. And the killer was there, looking at me, now, from among perhaps 40-50 men. Maybe even laughing at me. So for me, it was a personal affront I could not tolerate.

The why was for later.

I asked Shrimati to translate for me as I walked toward the first row.

"Blindfold me! That only the eyes of the god Shiva may see." I was learning the local patter.

The rows stopped moving and went silent.

With two rags wrapped about my eyes, Shrimati led me to the first row.

"Stretch out your right hands! Focus your minds on the knife of Haseeb Nabi! Concentrate your minds on it."

The killer would probably concentrate on anything but the magush's knife, and so should have no tremors.

I began to touch the extended wrists, detecting the tiny tremors of concentration. I suddenly felt the tremors of the man before me, though my hand was yet several inches from his.

"This man … who is he, Shrimati? He is special."

"You have found the wise man of Judpaw, a poet. He is blind." She paused. "I am impressed."

I continued down the first row, then on to the second. Another man I could detect from inches away, but he was a priest from the temple of Shiva. He had brought the sacred lotah bowl.

About a third of the way down the second row, I stopped before a man, a little leaner than the others. I felt nothing, at a distance or in touching his wrist. Down the sides of my nose I could see under the blindfold the repaired hems of his dirty baggy trousers, his filthy feet in worn sandals -- his *blistered feet*. I touched the next man whose tremors were easy to read, then reached back. Any man I identified might be killed on the spot. If I was wrong I could be a murderer myself.

He spoke a few words, angry words, which Shrimati translated.

"He wants to know why you stop before him. Why do you not seek the killer?"

Then I saw, understood, reached out and seized his arm, while tearing the blindfold from my eyes. I was stunned! I was looking into the eyes of the missionary James, his face, feet, hands and arms colored with a mahogany stain, but the faint lighter outlines of his glasses were still visible about his eyes.

He tried to pull away from me. "Damnit man, let me go," he whispered through clenched teeth. "These natives will kill us both! You're an Englishman, for God's sake. Let me go!"

I kicked his legs from under him sending him flat on his face.

"There is your killer, Shrimati, the missionary James," I said. "But he must stand trial. You cannot let these people tear him apart."

For a moment, a deep anger flared in her eyes. "He is the spy we have been seeking, who has betrayed our meetings to the British Raj. I would kill him myself!"

All beauty had vanished from her face, but then a moment, as the men swarmed around us, kicking at the sprawled figure of James, Shrimati raised her arms and her voice.

"Shiva has used Mr. Cumberland, an Englishman, to find the killer and spy, another Englishman. Let the English now show us their justice. The two English, the omen of the Great Nag." She looked at me, her eyes returning to normal. "You have served Shiva well, Mr. Cumberland. You are a friend of us, of the Shaivites, of the followers of the Lord Shiva. You will be protected. And that vermin," she tossed her hand toward James who was cowering in the dust behind upraised arms, "will be delivered as you wish.

"And we will be watching the British action, Mr. Cumberland," she said. "We will watch very closely."

#

Once James was secured in a locked compartment, Shrimati looked at me when we parted at the train station, a somber quizzical glance in her eyes. "You say justice, Mr. Cumberland? What justice? Which law? The law of our lands ... or of the British?

"Who is the real thief of Judpaw, Mr. Cumberland? One who comes to rob or even kill ... or one who comes to steal the culture and the dignity of the people?"

Shrimati Sarladevi vanished into the evening. "Open your mind, Mr. Cumberland. The mysteries of India are behind the eyes of her peoples ... not in hidden temples."

Her voice floated across the empty air.

#

Looking about the table at my Bombay hotel, the seven of us in immaculate evening dress, I said, "Well, gentlemen, it wasn't the power of Shiva that led me to

James; but when I couldn't detect anything at all in the man, and I saw that the tears in the man's trousers had been expertly repaired with a sewing machine, he didn't fit the pattern of the other thirty or so men I had already touched. And his feet were blistered. The feet of the natives are like slabs of iron. I knew then that he was the likely killer.

"When I threw him to the ground, his pistol fell from under his shirt. One shot had been fired."

From comments overheard that I had made during the voyage from England, I was thought to be a prospective British supporter of the Shaivite movement. My being able to travel widely through India without suspicion, coupled with my growing number of contacts at the highest level of the British government -- as carefully related in my publicity pieces -- made my potential involvement even more attractive to the activists. Thus Vicar Marley, who was a secret supporter, had arranged my meeting with the beautiful Shrimati Sarladevi.

#

Ah, but Imperial justice? The killer, Samuel James was an intelligence spy, put in place to track the development of the Shaivite organization. A harmless, ineffective, unseeing missionary was a perfect persona. James was, as an Imperial spy, quite fluent in the local languages and the culture. He was never prosecuted, and he and his wife vanished. Within days I was privately censured by the viceregal office for interference in Imperial affairs with a very blunt banishment order to leave India on the first ship to anywhere -- to Cairo, as it turned out.

Shrimati had admitted that the magush had used confederates in the various crowds to confirm his powers, to help authenticate his movements through the countryside under the eyes of the British agents.

But how Haseeb Nabi had read that Biblical passage Samuel James had selected, I have no idea.

I couldn't help reflecting on the faces of England I had encountered in India: Smythe-Howell, the naïve loyal Imperialist; the cruel angry face of the spy, Samuel James; the empty faces in the audiences at the cantonments where I performed before receiving my order of banishment. The English lived as on small islands in the vast sea of India, seduced by the fantasy of empire.

#

I had embarked from London an ardent Imperialist; I returned confused. Not a good mental state for a thought reader; even one whose handbills now read like the Arabian Nights.

AFTERTHOUGHT

Dr. John H. Watson, late of the Afghan army, wrote of one of my involvements in which he describes my first meeting with his close friend, Mr. Sherlock Homes. The circumstances occurred about two weeks after my Vienna encounter described earlier.

I will defer to Dr. Watson then to tell his tale of:

THE ADVENTURE OF
THE THOUGHTFUL MIND
READER

I hesitate to put my pen to paper. Across the room, Sherlock Holmes sits, brooding silently, beside the dying fire. His white hands lie listlessly on the arms of his rocking chair. He has no energy. He is not lethargic from drug use or from physical exertion -- but from debilitating regret.

Customarily, I wait a few months, even years, following the close of a case to allow for reflection on the events involved -- and to clarify any remaining uncertainties -- and, to allow time to plaster over, as it were, awkward memories. In the end, it is, quite naturally, Holmes who must give final assent to the publication of any of his cases. But in this instance, he has urged me to place these events before the public in the most urgent manner.

But, yet -- still I hesitate

#

It was an uncommon early October in 1885 for London. Early winter was present in the air, but this day, like the previous two days, was sunny and pleasant. Holmes had been in and out of our rooms, his face pleasantly flushed from the exercise and from the finding of some obscure book on Neolithic divinations.

Neither Holmes nor I had detected her presence on our steps, and I did not even hear her gentle knock. But Holmes was quickly at the door.

"Come in, please, Miss."

She was obviously nervous as she stepped into the room reeking of Holmes' first pipe of black shag of the morning mingled with the acrid reminders of his latest chemical experiments. The remains of my late morning breakfast had not yet been cleared from the table. Delicate in manner, she was dressed most fashionably, her face a painter's dream surrounded by chestnut curls.

"Thank you, Mr. Holmes," she said, her voice melodious but firm, looking over at me as I stood. "And you, sir, you are Dr. John H. Watson?"

I bowed. She may be nervous, but was certainly in full control of herself.

She seated herself in the chair indicated by Holmes, as he resumed his rocking chair, his long fingers pressed in an arch, his head laid back, his eyes half-lidded.

"How may I be of service to you on this beautiful day?" he asked. "I trust you were not injured in your accident."

She frowned, glanced about the room, then smiled. "No I was not, Mr. Holmes. But ... how? Ah, I think I see. The bruises on my wrist, the tear in my sleeve, and ... what have I missed?"

Homes smiled, immediately impressed. "Your scraped shoe. No lady with such a fashionable flair as you have would allow such imperfections for a moment. Thus all the indications must be very recent. Therefore something akin to an accident must have occurred in the cab that brought you to our door."

I expected a reaction of astonishment similar to that of most of our callers when Homes would read their life without asking questions; but the girl only smiled, her nervousness now gone.

"How very obvious and logical, sir," she said. "However, Mr. Cumberland has done more. He reads the thoughts of strangers while blindfolded; while you need your eyes for confirmation, Mr. Holmes.

"My name is Dorthea Richmond. I fear that I am to be killed and I want you to delay that event."

Her response had clearly marked Holmes. His eyes had widened slightly, he leaned forward.

"Delay, Miss Richmond," I said. "Do you not mean to prevent ...?"

She raised her hand. "Death will come, ultimately, Dr. Watson. I ask only that the event be delayed until I can know my grandchildren."

"Do you refer, Miss Richmond," Holmes said, rocking forward in his chair, "to Mr. Stuart C. Cumberland, the self-proclaimed thought reader?"

"Yes, Mr. Homes. Have you experienced his work?"

"No, Miss Richmond, neither Dr. Watson nor I have had that pleasure."

"My fiancée, Lord Ornum, and I are to attend a private soiree to be given by the Chevalier Cumberland tonight, in the ballroom at the Charing Cross Hotel. Please, gentlemen, be our guests. The thought reader will conduct an assassination tonight that you might find of interest."

I started at the casual way the young woman could speak of such horrors.

"It was Mr. Cumberland," she continued, "who detected the threat of murder against his Lordship … and me." Her generous smile suddenly shown brilliantly. "While blindfolded, Mr. Holmes. Blindfolded."

#

Stuart Charles Francis Cumberland was blindfolded. Along with two other gentlemen from among the fifty or so well-dressed men and women assembled in the opulent ballroom, I had helped to securely wrap a strip of black velvet over his remarkable blue eyes. Cumberland was a good-looking young man of medium height, thin mustache and fair hair oiled, combed back from his face and parted in the center. His voice was a pleasant tenor with a slight Cockney tone, his manner assured, not imperious. He had already found, found while blindfolded, Miss Richmond's hat pin that had been cleverly hidden on the very man who had served as the thought reader's silent guide.

Cumberland did not claim any occult or spiritualist powers, only that he could detect the thoughts of strangers through touching them, or by careful observation. After some ten minutes of leading the guide, Mr. David Neil Cameron, Esq., about the ballroom, Cumberland had suddenly stopped before us, dropped the barrister's hand, and stepped back.

He began to laugh. "Ah, my lords, ladies and gentlemen, you have striven to give me the most difficult test for a thought reader first off this evening. Bravo to you. To find something hidden on the very person whose slightest unconscious tremors are my guides to his mind and to the location of the concealed pin." Still blindfolded, Cumberland then reached out, his fumbling fingers first finding then going under Cameron's coat collar. He withdrew and held up the hidden hat pin, to enthusiastic applause -- applause in which both Holmes and I readily joined.

The accolade continued as the blindfolded thought reader, with some guidance, gallantly bowed before Miss Richmond to return her pin.

"An excellent demonstration of Dr. William B. Carpenter's theory of unconscious cerebration," murmured Holmes to me. "Excellent."

Still blindfolded, the thought reader wrote the serial number of a fifty pound note that he had never seen, that had been sealed inside an envelope by Major Alistair Gavin Martin, CBE, before the Major had even entered the hotel. The number was known only to Martin, whose right wrist Cumberland held with his left hand as he drew the numbers, holding a pen in his right hand, on a large sheet of paper hung on the wall. Holmes raised an eyebrow and nodded his head when Cumberland released the Major's hand as he wrote the last two digits. At Martin's confirmation that the serial number was correct as written, the audience gasped, then burst into another round of robust applause.

"Exceptional! Exceptional work, Watson. A man worth knowing," said Holmes, as the audience thundered their approval.

But now to the assassination, an imaginary one to be sure, but one colored by a brusque challenge from the young Lord Ornum, who had been noticeably piqued by

Cumberland's more than polite attentions to his beautiful fiancée. "Come, Mr. Cumberland," Lord Ornum said, standing, "I will wager a hundred pounds against your £10 that you cannot capture the assassin under my conditions."

His blindfold removed and still wiping perspiration from his face with a white silk handkerchief, Stuart Cumberland hesitated, looking over the suddenly stilled assemblage, then smiled and bowed toward Ornum.

"Your lordship's challenge and wager are accepted," he said. "With only one condition … which is, should I succeed, sir, I would ask your lordship to donate my one hundred pounds to the Children's Hospital." At that the audience burst into applause sprinkled with "bravo" and "marvelous" called out several times. Miss Richmond applauded enthusiastically, her smile enchanting.

Lord Ornum was noticeably grim faced.

A committee of three men was selected by Ornum as a waiter balancing a tray hurried up to respond to his sharp command.

"No fake blindfolds or handkerchiefs," declared his Lordship. Ornum, ignored the rumble of disapproval from the audience. He put his fingers into a small pot to withdraw what appeared to be a dollop of thick dough of some sort. "I will seal Mr. Cumberland's eyes with this pie dough, first; then his head will be wrapped securely with a thick black opaque bandage by Dr. McClure; finally an opaque black bag will be placed over his head and secured at his throat." At a sharp cry from Miss Richmond, Ornum smiled. "Please do not be alarmed. Mr. Cumberland will be able to breathe comfortably ... but he will not be able to cheat."

"My god, Ornum, you are going too far in this. This is savage!" an older gentleman stood and shouted. "We came to be entertained, man, not to witness a torture."

Cumberland raised his hand. "Thank you for your concern, sir, however it is his Lordship's wager, his conditions, so let it be."

Ornum and his three man committee worked diligently and in a few minutes the thought reader's sight was fully blocked. Ornum himself had slavered on a thick layer of dough over each of Cumberland's closed eyes.

"A bit excessive, Watson," whispered Holmes. "Lord Joseph is right. Wager or not, we are here only to be entertained, not to engage in clumsy psychical research."

Dr. McClure led Cumberland from the ballroom. Once the door was closed, Lord Ornum smiled. "Now, to the crime itself. I will ask Mr. Sherlock Holmes to guide us in selecting a victim, then a weapon and finally, let him be the assassin himself." He put out his hand toward Holmes, who stood and bowed to his lordship. "Surely, with his vast experience with the criminal world, Mr. Holmes can provide us all with unique insight into staging a proper crime."

Holmes looked toward Miss Richmond, who nodded, her lips pursed tightly.

#

She had explained to us that afternoon at Baker Street that Ornum was becoming deeply entangled with the spirits and the occult to where she feared his very sanity might be at risk. And that the threat to Ornum and to her had come from "out there", a strange sound and a vase fell to the floor, followed by a portrait of Miss Richmond falling from the wall. Then a mysterious note that Ornum had concealed, but that she recalled said that he would die where no human hand could have touched him.

"Why the threat, Miss Richmond?" Holmes had asked gently.

"Because I am unsuitable as a wife for an aristocrat, according to members of his family. My father, sir, runs a butcher shop. However, I believe the cause may be simpler than that. If Geoffry marries me then the future of the family fortune is, perhaps, impaired. But if Geoffry can be driven insane, or killed before the marriage then the family's financial interests are safe." Her wondrous face had gone cold.

#

Holmes selected Lord Joseph as the victim, then he walked to an alcove in the wall of the ballroom and returned with a small bronze bust of an angel.

"A weapon that is an unnoticed customary element of the premises is always an effective means of murder," he explained. "The police would be hard-pressed to discover such a weapon. It would be my preferred choice given the limited time of preparation." He walked back to return the bust to its place.

"Excellent, Mr. Holmes" said Lord Ornum. Nodding to a friend, he said, "Conrad, recall our celebrated thought reader."

Watching the young Mr. Cumberland was shocking, his head completely swathed in black, as he walked unsteadily toward us, stumbling even with Dr. McClure's hand on his arm; he seemed like a figure drawn from Sheridan Le Fanu's tortured imagination. I could see Holmes was angry, but there was nothing he could do. Cumberland had agreed.

"Here, sir, you stand before the audience who await your wonders," said Ornum.

His voice muffled, Cumberland said, "Please place someone of the committee at my side who knows the victim, weapon and the assassin ... that I might search his mind and ultimately ... identify the killer."

The audience was silent.

Captain Jonathan Gordon Mitchem, FRGS, touched Cumberland on his shoulder. "I am here, sir. You may begin."

Incredibly, Cumberland, though clearly blinded, led, even dragged Mitchem behind him and dodging through the audience, knocked over a chair, almost ran to Lord Joseph. He placed his hand on his Lordship's shoulder.

"The victim," the thought reader said loudly through his black bindings to the immediate cheers of the audience.

Holmes smiled. "Impressive, Watson, truly impressive."

"Now the weapon," declared Cumberland. "Concentrate, Captain, on the weapon and its placement. Concentrate. I cannot reach ... touch your mind unless you cooperate."

Cumberland walked rapidly, almost dragging the Captain behind him, in a circle in the open dance floor as the murmuring audience all rose to watch. Ornum was grinning with satisfaction. Then the thought reader moved rapidly in a larger circle. He stopped, clearly uncertain. "Ah," said the thought reader, "the assassin has cleverly camouflaged the weapon in some way. Concentrate, Captain."

Suddenly, Cumberland twisted around and walked quickly toward the alcove, actually leaving the bewildered Captain standing several paces behind him.

"Stunning, Watson. What is this?" Holmes frowned, stepping aside to gain a fuller view through the agitated crowd. "What is he doing?"

When Cumberland came to the wall, he began to run his hands along it, up, across, down, up again. "It's here," he shouted from under the thick hood around his head. "It's here somewhere!"

Abruptly, he stopped as though he had received some further revelation. The Captain walked up and stood three or four feet behind the thought reader, saying and doing nothing.

"Concentrate, Captain … please concentrate … *from where you are … from where you stand!*" Cumberland's probing left hand discovered the edge of the alcove, then he moved both hands about touching the angel, the plinth on which it stood on, the wall behind. Then he stopped. All silence, no one moved, the audience held its collective breath. The thought reader slowly reached out and grasped the bronze angel. He held it up high. "Here! Here is the weapon! An inspired choice by the assassin!"

The audience exploded in applause and cheering.

"Now, if the Captain will kindly guide me back to the audience, I can begin the final step … the identification of the killer."

Standing again where he had started with the Captain's wrist in his left hand, Cumberland began to walk slowly back toward the alcove, then turned back, as though following invisible footprints, back toward the audience. The Captain caught him when Cumberland nearly tripped and fell across a rug.

"Thank you, sir. I am not clairvoyant, I cannot see through pie dough and blindfolds, so please forgive me if I step on your feet."

Ornum was no longer grinning. He was troubled in some way, I could see that.

Cumberland dropped the Captain's hand and stepped toward a gentleman who at first attempted to get out of his way. "No, sir, stay. I will pass you." Cumberland moved on to the next row of chairs, then turned toward where Holmes and I were sitting. I began to get a very uneasy feeling. I knew of no scientific theories that could fully account for everything we had experienced this evening.

The thought reader moved slowly down the row, asking a lady's pardon as he stepped on the hem of her gown. Then, only a chair away from Holmes, Cumberland said, "Sir, will you rise that I might pass you." The man immediately stood and pushed his chair back.

Cumberland finally stood, his head encased in black, sweat dripping from his fingertips, next to Sherlock Holmes. He reached out his hand, then paused. "If I am wrong at this point, my lords, ladies and gentlemen, then Lord Ornum wins his wager, even if I were to find the true assassin later. But if I touch the assassin now, then I ..." He placed his hand firmly on Holmes' shoulder. "This is the foul fiend who committed our imaginary murder!"

With the burst of applause, Holmes rose, gripped Cumberland's sweaty hand and said, "My warmest congratulations, Mr. Cumberland, a truly impressive demonstration!"

When all of the bag, bindings and pie dough were finally removed from Cumberland's sweat polished face, the audience rose as one to applaud. To his credit, Lord Ornum bowed toward Cumberland and with a fine flourish, presented him with a hundred pound note.

Cumberland, still wiping his face with his handkerchief, returned the bow, took the note and presented it to the Director of the Children's Hospital who was present. "From his Lordship and I, sir, with our warmest compliments."

#

His Lordship had invited Holmes and I, and then stepped to one side to explicitly include Stuart Cumberland, to join him and his fiancée in the library at his notable home in Belgrave Square. He had taken the crystal bottle from his butler and had insisted on pouring the cognac himself. At the butler's withdrawal, Ornum raised his glass to the four seated before the richly carved red marble fireplace.

"Thank you for coming. And, Mr. Cumberland, please accept my apologies for my brusque behavior toward you at Charing Cross. I was profoundly impressed by your performance. I have experienced so much fraud and swindle in my search for answers to the great question of our time that my frustrations evaded my control. Again, my apology."

Lord Ornum's family cognac floated across my tongue as an angel's touch.

"Your Lordship," said Cumberland, "you have no apology to make. Your conditions though difficult, were fair, in my judgment. You did force me to plunge deeper into my art than at any other time, so I stand in your debt for the experience."

"Hear, hear," I said, raising my glass. "A most gallant response."

Ornum took a step toward Cumberland who immediately rose, extended his hand to the thought reader. "I certainly agree with Dr. Watson, sir," he said.

As Cumberland resumed his green-leather wing chair, he said, "Your Lordship's collection of books on the search for the answer to life after death is extraordinary. There are titles up there that I know of only by rumor. My sincere admiration, sir.

"And if I may, sir, how many servants do you have in the house?"

Ornum raised an eyebrow at the question. "Mr. Cumberland, please consider this entire library as yours to use at any time." He raised his hand to the shelves of the expansive library filled with books and scrolls of all sizes surrounding us on all four walls which soared to the high gilded ceiling where they joined a vast mural which displayed ancient Greek sages disputing among themselves. "I shall so instruct my staff ... which consists of a butler, a cook, three chamber maids downstairs and two maids upstairs ... and outside help as necessary."

Cumberland nodded. "My deepest thanks, your Lordship, for opening this library to me. I intend to put it to work with some alacrity."

I noted Holmes' half-smile. I waited -- not long.

"Would it be possible, your Lordship, to see the threatening note you received?" asked Holmes. "However it may have been delivered."

158

Lord Ornum withdrew a folded square of cream stationary from his waistcoat and gave it to Holmes. Both Cumberland and I stood behind Holmes' chair to read over his shoulder. The ink, though dry, still glistened. The paper was of obvious quality.

There were but two lines, written in elegant script:

You have violated the trust of the spirits, Ornum.

You will die where no human hand can touch you.

Holmes removed his glass from his vest to closely examine the ink and writing, then both sides of the paper. "Most interesting, your Lordship. There are only two shops in London who sell this ink which is made in Bombay. It contains tiny thin silica crystals to create the sheen upon drying. The paper is another problem. Though of most interesting quality, it lacks the paper maker's customary mark which was cut off here." He tapped one edge. "So we have our work cut out to discover who prepared the note, but it should not require more than half a day at most." Holmes stood. "May I keep this, your Lordship?"

"Certainly."

"Then Watson, you and I have work to do. My thanks, your Lordship, for your kind hospitality." He bowed to Dorthea Richmond. "We shall gain our answers as quickly as possible, Miss Richmond."

Lord Ornum and his fiancée escorted Holmes, Cumberland, and I to the great carved oak door of his imposing home. As we were shaking hands, Cumberland said, "May I suggest, your Lordship, that when you accompany Miss Richmond to her rooms at the Savoy, that you take a room there yourself until this business is resolved? I have a very uneasy feeling … call it a thought reader's sense … a very uneasy presentment that you should not be in this house tonight, nor any night, until the killers are captured."

I had noted Cumberland's scrutiny of the servants as we had been escorted into the library, coupled with his question to Ornum.

Miss Richmond gasped. Her face drained of color. She grasped her fiancée's arm tighter. "Geoffry …!"

"Your thoughts, Mr. Holmes," Ornum asked, his face grim.

"While I respect Mr. Cumberland's assessment, your Lordship," said Holmes, "I cannot agree to its necessity. I will have the name of the purchaser of the ink and paper by tomorrow, noon at the latest. With that identity, we can enlist the police to track him down for questioning."

"Very well, Mr. Holmes. Mr. Cumberland, thank you for your warning and concern, but I will rely on Mr. Holmes's well-known acumen with criminal matters."

#

Holmes had been gone when I arose the following morning. He had returned as I finished my kippers, his face flushed with satisfaction. "Sir Michael Hayes-Ornum, Watson, bought the ink eight days ago. Sir Michael is his Lordship's uncle and would inherit the Ornum estate on his Lordship's demise. We have him Watson! Sir Michael bought the paper at Sloan's five days ago, I have the proof here." The police, within less than an hour, confirmed that Sir Michael had left Euston Station for Glasgow at 8:47am, the previous day. Immediate telegrams were sent to the Glasgow police.

We returned to Baker Street from Euston Station with some satisfaction, particularly Holmes. "I bear Mr. Cumberland no ill will, Watson; but his premature warning to Lord Ornum unduly upset Miss Richmond. The evidence was there, it was only a matter of knowledge of the inks and paper, of which I have written three monographs, and the immediate support of the police and the situation was resolved."

There was a note waiting for us at Baker Street requesting Sherlock Holmes immediate presence at Belgrave Square. Lord Ornum had been found dead with no marks on his body, in a locked windowless strong room bolted from the inside.

His Lordship had been found at 9:00am.

#

A grim-faced uniformed police sergeant stood at the strong room door while Detective Hall Hopkins, whom neither Holmes nor I had ever met, was taking testimony from servants. But none of the family looked anywhere except at Sherlock Holmes whom Dorthea Richmond had immediately summoned.

She had also sent for Stuart Cumberland who stood now behind Holmes as Holmes knelt down beside the young lord's body. The thought reader, dressed in a bespoke dark grey sack suit of the latest fashion, looked carefully around the white painted strong room, its four shelves of leather-backed account books, family memorabilia together with three large locked dispatch boxes, at the opened door and then back at the body, then around the room again.

His jaw noticeably tightened.

Cumberland knelt down beside Holmes while I also knelt on the opposite side of the young lord. His Lordship was still dressed as we had last seen him the previous night. His final expression of terrified agony was frightening to behold.

"A nasty business, Mr. Holmes, and … so unnecessarily dramatic," said the thought reader, quietly.

Holmes, his brow knitted, looked over at me. "Watson, what do you see?" He turned to Cumberland and nodded. "My thoughts exactly, Mr. Cumberland. We need to speak with Miss Richmond in private."

Cumberland gave a slight nod.

I had noted that once Cumberland had quickly examined the dead body, he searched the faces of the people surrounding us -- family and servants. There was a certain, ah, even queer reaction on the part of two or three, particularly two maids, who seemed to step back to strive to avoid the thought reader's glance. They were believers in his powers, that much was certain.

I looked up.

"There are no apparent physical marks or wounds, thus the source of death must be something else. A form of strychnine poisoning, Holmes, could produce the stressed facial features, but he clearly saw something that was horrific," I offered. "There seems more than just one poison in this case ... as though there was a second poison."

As Stuart Cumberland stood, he said, "A second poison. Well said, Dr. Watson. A most thoughtful insight." He glanced again at the people surrounding us.

#

"Because the proof of telepathy, of thought transference beyond the normal senses, is the first firm step to scientifically proving survival after death, Mr. Homes," Dorthea Richmond answered Holmes' question. "As Professor William Barrett has pointed out," she continued, "in his public lectures and his documented work with the remarkable Creery sisters, and the demonstrations of Mr. Blackburn and Mr. Smith, as well as other work of the Society for Psychical Research."

The coal fire in the carved red marble fireplace had just been lit by a maid who had then immediately withdrawn. "Geoffry had become obsessed with life after death. He so wanted to know what lay beyond what we know as life. Thus his interest in the demonstrations of Mr. Cumberland, with his deep desire to probe the limits of Mr. Cumberland's abilities." She turned to Stuart Cumberland and reached out her hands, which he took gently in his. "He so wanted to know, Mr. Cumberland … he had to know" --

tears began to flow gently down her cheeks -- "he had to know how close you were to the enchanted boundary. Had you actually crossed it? Were you the first to do it? He had to know."

Cumberland was clearly touched by Miss Richmond's grief.

"Last night," suggested Holmes, gently moving the discussion back to the murder. "Last night after we had left?"

Wiping her eyes with a blue lace handkerchief, Miss Richmond said, "Geoffrey became feverish with excitement. He spoke of commissioning, asking Mr. Cumberland to participate in a series of careful studies of telepathy, both with and without physical contact, and of examinations beyond the five senses. To go further than the Committee for Thought Transference of the Society for Psychical Research has yet gone.

"Perhaps, he speculated, delving into physical phenomena, of what he called action at a distance, even Mr. William Crookes' *psychic force*." She tried to smile toward Cumberland, "He would have paid you, sir, a thousand pounds or even more to devote two to three months of your time to the study, regardless of the results. He viewed your time as uniquely valuable."

"And?" asked Holmes.

Miss Richmond hesitated. "He bluntly asked me if I believed in an after-life, but one accessible to the living. That was the first time he had so closely questioned me. He, strangely, seemed to make it ... almost a condition of continuing our relationship. The butcher shop in my life had never before come between us, but now it seemed to appear as out of thin air."

"Your answer, if I may ask?" said Cumberland. "Please be aware, Miss Richmond, that I also have a butcher shop in my life that I have had to conceal behind a public persona suitable for entering salons, as these." He tossed his hand toward the walls of the library. "The Khedive of Egypt, Lord Kitchener, and the Grand Duke Michael of Russia would never have allowed a mere son of a butcher shop clerk to stand before them, regardless of any wonders performed. English society is no different. The riches of the Queen's Empire are not equally accessible."

Her smile, though weak, was pretty to see. "I said, Mr. Cumberland … I answered a firm no. But that I was eager to see proof that I was wrong."

"A brave answer," said Holmes, as Cumberland nodded his agreement.

#

Cumberland, Holmes and I rejoined Inspector Hall Hopkins in the library after he had finished his private questioning of Miss Richmond. She had left to return to her temporary rooms at the Savoy Hotel. Her saddened wondrous face and weak wave of farewell gripped my heart.

Hopkins smiled when shaking hands with Holmes. "My colleagues speak very highly of you, Mr. Holmes. I am frank to say I welcome your insights into this strange business." But Hopkins' smile vanished when he acknowledged Stuart Cumberland. His voice quickly became heated. "I'll not have you trying to gain unsightly publicity at police expense from this sad affair, Mr. Cumberland. I know you conjurors too well. And I have read magicians' unhelpful comments and experienced your snide arrogance in the *Times*, *The Saturday Review* and other journals regarding the recent series of dynamite outrages in the East End." He then acknowledged me and we all sat in front of the red marble fireplace once again.

"Dr. Wynter agrees with your observations, Dr. Watson. He will perform blood tests to determine what else, other than the strychnine, might be there."

"But how he lies in a locked room is outside my experience, gentlemen. I would appreciate any insights you could provide from your own varied experiences."

Pursing his lips, Cumberland spoke first. "If I were to have been the killer intent on presenting an occult form of murder, to match the earlier written threats, then I would have given his Lordship the first poison and suggested something that would have led my victim into the strong room, where I would have presented him with the second poison, something to challenge his sanity. Once he was dead in the strong room, I would have raised the inside bolt on the door to a vertical position and held it, barely, in place with a wad of paper wedged between it and the door. Then I would have sharply pulled the door closed which would have dislodged the wad and allowed the bolt to fall into place, thus securing the door from the inside … the work being due, obviously, to the miserable spirits."

Cumberland's face was cold as he leaned back in his chair.

After a brief moment, Holmes nodded his agreement, while Hopkins asked, "How is it, Mr. Cumberland, that the means of murder come so quickly to your mind?"

"Because, Inspector," Cumberland responded, his face deeply clouded, "because I encountered just such a vile murder not more than two weeks ago in Vienna. There the 'spiritual circumstances' had been created by an accident; here, however, they are clearly intentional."

Holmes was quiet, his manner markedly subdued in contrast to our active morning. But clearly Sir Michael could not have been the killer. Also clearly, Cumberland's warning to the young Lord of the previous evening was weighing heavily on his mind.

"May I ask, Inspector,' said Cumberland, "that you arrange all the servants in the entrance hall in a rough line? I should like to look into their minds."

Hopkins jaw dropped. "What?" he snapped. "This is a murder investigation, sir, not a music hall audition!"

Holmes raised his hand. "I should like to see Mr. Cumberland's experiment, Inspector," he said quietly, his face somber.

Hopkins dropped his jaw a second time, his eyes wide.

#

Each of the house staff, from the butler, Blake, to the two Chinese assistants in the kitchen stood in a rough line in the entrance hall. Their expressions ranged from the Chinese indifference to the taut concern of the maids.

"I am going to probe each of your minds," said Stuart Cumberland, his eyes sweeping slowly across the rank that faced him. "When I come before you, please extend your right hand. I will hold that hand for a moment then pass on. Thank you for your cooperation."

Hopkins and two of his men stood behind Cumberland with disbelief evident on their faces.

Holmes was silent, his jaw set.

I had never before seen defeat in his face.

Cumberland moved from the butler, to the downstairs maids whose hands he held slightly longer than that of Blake. He started to move on to the cook, only to turn back to the maids again. Then he moved on to cook and her Chinese helpers. He stood for a moment at the end of the line, his frown deep.

"I can dismiss Blake ... the cook with her assistants." Those named immediately left the hall. "And both upstairs maids may leave." The two young women looked at each with relief and walked rapidly away. The three remaining maids were clearly intimidated. When Cumberland began to approach them, they all retreated a step. One, Susan, held her hands to her face as if to hide herself.

Cumberland stood quietly before the three young women, then stepped forward, his right hand extended to the maid in the center, Hattie, who immediately stepped back. Her face became contorted with anguish. Hattie looked at the two girls beside her as if pleading ....

"Hattie, please take my hand," said Cumberland, firmly, but gently.

"He said he would marry me!" Hattie suddenly exploded, her face drained of color. "Not that butcher shop bitch, but me! Me! My Pa was a barrister before the drink got him, a barrister not a butcher! Nelson said only the spirits would be blamed. No one could see how Geoffry was killed, no one. Not even the holy Holmes!

"My brother, Nelson, knew about Sherlock Holmes, read everything about his methods." She was calmer now, her face distorted only by hate, not desperation. "So Nelson got the ink and paper. He knew Mr. Holmes would seize on that … would follow that like a cat after a mouse. He bought it using Sir Michael's address. Nelson knew the police would know nothing; they were no concern."

Hopkins' face went red with anger and astonishment.

"If Geoffry wasn't going to wed me, then he wasn't going to wed anyone! Nelson promised me.

"But we was ready for Mr. Holmes, but we didn't plan on *him* being in on it! Him!" She jabbed her fist at the thought reader, then covered her face with her hands and began to weep.

Stuart Cumberland stepped back. "Inspector, I believe the situation is now entirely yours."

Holmes was silent for a moment, then he stepped up to Cumberland, extended his hand. "My congratulations, Mr. Cumberland, I have received a most valuable lesson this morning. A lesson that requires my detailed and humble reflection."

The police captured Nelson Godwin at Charing Cross Station. He had several pieces of Ornum silver along with £600 in cash all taken from the strong room. He and Hattie were to be together on the boat train to the Continent. He was confident that they would be out of reach before Holmes and the police would realize that Sir Michael was not the killer. It had been Hattie who had beguiled Ornum into the strong room. His Lordship was going to give Hattie a silver and gold broach for her silence about their affair. Instead she gave him the second poison which Dr. Wynter had not yet identified.

They had not reckoned with the presence of Stuart Cumberland, Hattie had said, as Hopkins took her under arrest, "If we knowed Mr. Cumberland would be involved, we never would have tried."

#

I laid my pen aside.

"Finished, Watson?" Sherlock Holmes asked, his head against the chair, his eyes closed.

"Yes."

"Then don't delay."

A Closing Thought

There are other tales, naturally. A thought reader by the nature of his craft is often involved with bizarre events. There is, for example, the odd situation I had with the young Khedive, Abbas II Hilmi Bey, who has been mentioned once or twice above. The young ruler brought inexperience and an implacable hatred for everything British to the Egyptian throne. I had just been thrown out of India by the British Raj for meddling in Imperial affairs; and very nearly accomplished the same feat in Cairo -- but with a deadly Khedivian twist.

But all that is for our next meeting at the Bloody Two Squires pub.

Until that time, I raise my glass to you, filled with the finest Scotch whiskey on earth, with the sincere toast:

May your thoughts always be pleasant

And -- unreadable.

Cheers!

Yours sincerely,
Stuart C. Cumberland

A BRIEF BIBLIOGRAPHY

OF THOUGHT READING

Stuart Cumberland's thought reading was first created by the American, John Randall Brown, on a Monday morning in a Chicago saloon in 1873, and is still being practiced today. Should you want to learn of its subtle techniques, confounding difficulties, and sharp limitations, the following books would prove useful.

Dariel Fitzkee, *Contact Mind Reading Expanded*, 3rd edition, 1970. Note his description of the neutral subject scenario.

S. Edward Dexter, *Entertaining with Contact Mind Reading*, 1952. A good discussion of programming a performance of Contact Mindreading.

Satori, *Making Contact*, 1998. This is the most detailed description available on achieving success in Contact Mindreading.

As noted in these stories of Stuart Cumberland, and in these three books, even with your knowing, strange events are certain to happen.

OTHER BOOKS BY
BARRY H. WILEY

The
Adventures in Second Sight
Series

Set in the turbulent final decade of the 19th century, *Adventures in Second Sight* tells of the adventurous life of Kyame Piddington as she encounters bank robbers, killers, con men, Jadoowallahs, and the hatchet men of the Bing On tong as beginning at age eleven she travels the American West with her father as The Impossible Piddingtons ... and the consistent rejection by polite society because Kyame is only a theatre girl.

Kyame's later travels take her beyond America to England, France, Hawaii and the islands of the South Seas during which she encounters historical personages as Paul Gauguin; the Prince of Wales; Queen Victoria; the greatest American mesmerist, J. W. Cadwell; British Prime Minister, Lord Salisbury; and others, lesser known, but very much historically real.

Book 1, *Revelations of the Impossible Piddingtons.* http://amazon.com/dp/B003VP9W6E

It is1890-95. "Kyame seems a girl ready for her dragon tattoo ...," according to Kirkus Media. Continuing, Kirkus says, "Wiley deftly renders the period atmosphere, attitudes, action and dialogue ... Kyame could develop a loyal following of readers of all ages and sexes ..." And regarding the novel, Kirkus describes it as, "A magical concept and a miraculous heroine keep the pages turning ..." Published 2010. Available in print and e-book formats on Amazon.

Book 2, *The Shadow of the Tiger.*

http://amazon.com/dp/B00LP287CK

It is 1896. All the British intelligence agents in Southern France have been killed. Even their replacements are murdered within a few days of their appearing. Lord Salisbury, British Prime Minister, appeals to President Grover Cleveland for assistance. With no American intelligence presence in Europe, Cleveland must turn to a unique informal group called the Anglo-Oriental Insurance Co. that reports to Richard Olney, his Secretary of State. Though seventeen, only Kyame Piddington has the unique skills needed to confront N, the Imperial German Intelligence Service, as Kaiser Wilhelm II pushes to control the Mediterranean Sea and threaten British control of the Suez Canal. Kyame must utilize all of her strange skills, including the yellow ruhmal of the Thuggee cult, in her battle to understand and stop the German threat. Kyame also encounters a young Frenchman who captures her heart only to disappear. Published 2014. Available in print and e-book formats on Amazon.

Book 3 **Pi Ying Xi:** *The Shadow Play.* Set in 1897 in San Francisco, Honolulu, Cairo, and Tahiti. In-progress.

The Thought Reader Craze, McFarland, 2012.

A non-fiction study of the intense search by scientists, academics and others to establish telepathy as a fact of human nature -- and perhaps the first scientific proof of life-after-death. The book also tells the story of the men, woman and, occasionally, children who so successfully hoaxed the scientists; as well as the parallel story of the creation of the one-man minding act one Monday morning in 1873 in a Chicago saloon. The stage performers used the scientists to gain public credit, while the scientists used the performers to maintain public interest. In the end, the performers gained and lost fortunes, while the scientists gained and lost reputations. Winner of the 2013 Melbourne Christopher Literary Award of the Society of American Magicians.

The Thought Reader Craze is available on Amazon, Barnes & Noble, the McFarland website and in local bookstores, in both print and e-book formats.

The Indescribable Phenomenon: the life and mysteries of Anna Eva Fay, Hermetic Press, 2005.

The biography of the woman whom, in 1909, magician Harry Houdini called, "the greatest female mystifier". In 1875 Annie was publicly acclaimed by scientists and psychical researchers in Great Britain as a genuine psychic, capable of exerting a "non-human force at a distance"; while in 1877, detective Allan Pinkerton called her, "… a woman possessing a terribly fascinating power and capable of any devilish human accomplishment."

Raised in conditions of near slavery in northeastern Ohio, five feet tall, blonde, blue-eyed, Annie Fay was the quintessential con woman. Though a fake, she became celebrated as one of the premier spirit mediums of her day; when the profits from her spirits began to fade, in 1894 Annie went on the vaudeville stage doing what she had been doing in the séance room. She stole the mindreading act of magician Samri S. Baldwin to fill out her act, and became celebrated as a greater showman than Houdini himself. Baldwin himself said publicly that she performed the act better than he did. When Anna Eva Fay died in 1927, she was eulogized in the New York *Times*. The biography was considered for a film by Walden Media, but the project never moved ahead. Available in print on Amazon, and from the publisher, Hermetic Press in Seattle, WA www.hermeticpress.com

A Spirit of Fraud, 2013.

Set in 1876. A British occult Brotherhood under the apparent direction of the Archangel Uriel plans to seize defenseless America in the waning months of the Grant administration. Only the celebrated spirit medium, Annie Eva Fay, detects the threatening presence of Uriel's minions. Gaining the help of the Pinkertons, Annie moves to stop the Brotherhood. But Annie's spirits are all fake. Is the Archangel a fake as well? And will there be time enough for Annie to learn the truth?

The novel was reviewed October, 2014, on *Kings River Life Magazine* (www.kingsriverlife.com) with a comparison to *The DaVinci Code.*

A Spirit of Fraud is available in e-book format on Kobo, Barnes & Noble, and Apple iBookstore, and in e-book and print on Amazon.

Beyond The Tempest, a sorcerous tale of Bermuda, 2014.

Bermuda. Pink sand, exotic beauty, mysterious history, a three billion dollar national debt, and a per capita murder rate twice that of New York even with the most draconian gun control law in the Western world: Ten years in prison without parole for possession of any gun, or any part of a gun. In *Beyond The Tempest,* the real Bermuda is a principal character in the novel, not simply a tourist backdrop.

Set in contemporary times, the novel tells the story of mentalist and former physicist, Kaarin Larsson, who is booked at the last minute into a venture capital conference in Bermuda to replace Tony DiMarco, celebrated memory expert who has been murdered twice, shot with a .32 and a .41 magnum at the same time in a deserted Bermuda cemetery. DiMarco's killers thus were risking hard time just holding the guns. But why two killers?

Kaarin is attacked by two killers her first night in Bermuda, one with the .41 and one with a knife. She knows no one in Bermuda – why her?

Together with Inspector Keith Haggard of the Bermuda Police Service, she searches for answers. Why are her friends Serreta and Sugar Alberts, magicians currently performing at the Pink Sands in Bermuda, also targeted?

But the constant underlying question that torments her nights, and her unguarded moments: is she human?

Note: Research for *Beyond The Tempest* included interviewing the Bermuda Commissioner of the Police Service, which resulted in his assigning an officer to show the author Bermuda as the police see it -- a remarkably fascinating afternoon in paradise.

Beyond The Tempest is distributed in e-book format through Smashwords to Barnes & Noble, Kobo, and Apple iBookstore. E-book and print versions are available through Amazon and local bookstores.

For more information on the stories and books of Barry H. Wiley visit his website at www.barrywiley.com Follow his Author's Page and his blog "Plotting the Impossible" on Goodreads.